PUFFIN BOOKS

Listening for Lucca

As a little girl, Suzanne LaFleur vacationed in Maine with her family and loved to search for treasures on the beach. She still visits Maine at least once a year. She is also the author of *Love, Aubrey* and *Eight Keys*. Visit her online at suzannelafleur.com.

D1389300

Books by Suzanne LaFleur

EIGHT KEYS
LISTENING FOR LUCCA
LOVE, AUBREY

Listening for Lucca

SUZANNE LaFLEUR

PUFFIN

PUFFIN BOOKS

Published by the Penguin Group
Penguin Books Ltd, 80 Strand, London WC2R ORL, England
Penguin Group (USA) Inc., 375 Hudson Street, New York, New York 10014, USA
Penguin Group (Canada), 90 Eglinton Avenue East, Suite 700, Toronto, Ontario, Canada M4P 2Y3
(a division of Pearson Penguin Canada Inc.)
Penguin Ireland, 25 St Stephen's Green, Dublin 2, Ireland (a division of Penguin Books Ltd)
Penguin Group (Australia), 707 Collins Street, Melbourne, Victoria 3008, Australia
(a division of Pearson Australia Group Pty Ltd)
Penguin Books India Pvt Ltd, 11 Community Centre, Panchsheel Park, New Delhi – 110 017, India
Penguin Group (NZ), 67 Apollo Drive, Rosedale, Auckland 0632, New Zealand
(a division of Pearson New Zealand Ltd)
Penguin Books (South Africa) (Pty) Ltd, Block D, Rosebank Office Park, 181 Jan Smuts Avenue,
Parktown North, Gauteng 2193, South Africa

Penguin Books Ltd, Registered Offices: 80 Strand, London WC2R ORL, England

puffinbooks.com

Published in the United States by Wendy Lamb Books, an imprint of Random House Children's
Books, a division of Random House, Inc., New York 2013
Published simultaneously in Great Britain by Puffin Books 2013

001

Copyright © Suzanne LaFleur, 2013
All rights reserved

The moral right of the author has been asserted

Set in Goudy
Printed in Great Britain by Clays Ltd, St Ives plc

British Library Cataloguing in Publication Data
A CIP catalogue record for this book is available from the British Library

HARDBACK
ISBN: 978–0–141–33607–7

www.greenpenguin.co.uk

MIX
Paper from
responsible sources
FSC
www.fsc.org FSC™ C018179

Penguin Books is committed to a sustainable
future for our business, our readers and our planet.
This book is made from Forest Stewardship
Council™ certified paper.

ALWAYS LEARNING   **PEARSON**

For my chickpea

1

I'm obsessed with abandoned things.

Left-behind things, unwanted things. Forgotten things.

When Lucca and I got to the park, a small lamb waited
on a bench.

The lambie was stuffed and half-full of plastic beans and
fluff. He was gray and worn; chew marks creased his nose.
He was small enough to hold in one hand.

No sign of the lamb's owner. There was only one other
person at the park. He wore a top hat and formal jacket,
very hot clothes for sweltering July. He was reading the
paper, and every once in a while he took out a pocket
watch to check the time. I could see him only out of the
corner of my eye; I didn't want to be caught glancing his
way. I wasn't sure if he was really there, but people dress
in all kinds of funny ways around here, so I tried to tell
myself he was just someone in old-fashioned clothes. Not
something else.

Because from time to time, I get these glimpses of things, almost like . . .

The lamb, I reminded myself. I sat down beside it and waited. I'd let Lucca play for half an hour; if no one came for the lamb by then, I would take it home.

That was always the gamble. What if someone came back and their special thing was gone?

But I always think: they *forgot*. The lamb could sit there, fade in the sun and rot in the rain. It might take the owner ages to remember that he'd even had a lamb. Then it would be too late and all a waste.

My collection of rescued things drives Mom crazy. I started it about a year and a half ago, sometime after Lucca stopped talking. Mom used to tell me not to bring home junk I'd found, but I insisted that these carefully selected items weren't junk, though I couldn't explain it any better than that. I cleaned them and set them neatly on my shelf and made sure dust didn't gather on them. How was it that they had come to be lost?

Sometimes things need rescuing.

Mom seemed to be hoping that when we moved I wouldn't take my collection with me. She'd limited the number of boxes I could use, thinking I might pick other things instead, but it was actually the first thing I packed.

"Siena, what if you don't have room for the important things now?"

"This *is* an important thing. I'll leave behind my winter clothes if I have to."

Mom had let out an exasperated sigh. Moving to our own house on the New England coast would not be the time to leave winter clothes behind. I knew that would push her buttons.

I also knew what Dad had told me, which was that the moving truck would be huge. So Mom was full of it. We could bring everything we wanted. Dad had said so.

I watched Lucca climb up the green-painted bars and zip down the slide. He made some kind of low superhero noises and zoomed around the climbing structure on foot. "Whoosh, shwoosh, whoosh."

This time was the last Lucca would play here. I'd played in this park every day when I was little, too. It hadn't changed, except for the color of the painted bars, from orange to beige and green. I knew every corner, from the cozy hiding spot under the slide to where to turn on the sprinklers in the summer. I was tempted to go for one final climb-and-slide myself, but I stayed put, watching. Lucca didn't mind playing alone. Maybe he even preferred it.

I kept track of the half hour on my watch.

"Come on, Lucca. It's time to go home."

The word *home* hung in the air, as if testing itself.

I scooped up the lamb. Lucca pointed, asking about it.

"It's dirty," I explained. "We can't play with it."

When I didn't hand it over, he shrugged and took my other hand. We walked back to our apartment.

In my room, I found the box with the other collected items in it. A pocket watch with a broken face. A Brooklyn library card that said *Hannah Stone* in little-kid writing. A shovel-and-bucket pair from the beach. Three unmatched earrings. A participation ribbon for an unknown event. A silver spoon, except it probably wasn't real silver, because it didn't tarnish. And a hundred other things. I dropped in the lamb and folded the cardboard flaps back down.

I looked at my life, packed up in a dozen boxes. My life, and all these little pieces of other lives. I was their protector. They wouldn't be left behind again.

Our apartment would become an abandoned thing. One too big to collect.

The movers were coming in the morning.

• • •

The upstairs hallway has the glow of daylight but no direct sunshine. The ocean breeze blows in through the open windows of the four bedrooms. I put my hand on the banister and follow the railing to the stairs and then down. At the bottom, I look right and left into living rooms on either side and step through the grand front doorway onto a painted wooden porch. From there I can see the ocean. Everything's calm and beautiful, but the breeze chills my arms and makes the hair on them stand up.

I awoke, still in my bed in Brooklyn.

Back around the time Lucca had stopped talking and I'd started collecting, I'd also started dreaming about this house, this big old house by the sea.

Today we were going there.

4

Mom was arguing with Lucca over sealing up his toys in boxes.

"But that's how they'll ride in the truck to our new house," she said. Then, "But we have to close them in so they stay nice and safe. We have to shut the boxes!"

Arguing between them is Mom getting louder and louder, and Lucca not saying anything but using his body to show what he wants. I didn't go into the tiny office that we'd converted into his bedroom, but from Mom's shouts of "Lucca, get up! Get off!" I pictured him slung across the boxes. I guess I wasn't the only one trying Mom's patience during the packing process.

I got dressed, grabbed my notebook and music, and yelled to Mom that I was going.

We'd made this deal: I didn't want to see our apartment empty and abandoned, and Mom wanted as few people as possible underfoot, so she told me I could sit in the coffee shop on the corner until it was time to go.

"Bye!" I yelled.

"Wait!" She hurried after me. "Here's a twenty. And take your brother!"

I hadn't expected that. But Lucca's tiny sneakers pounded to catch up, and soon his hand was in mine.

At the coffee shop, I set up Lucca at a table by the window. It was so early no one else was sitting down yet, just getting coffees to go. I bought juice and a muffin for me and a slice of some kind of loaf cake and a yogurt for Lucca. He ate happily for a long time while I wrote and listened to my music. Eventually he finished eating, so I tore pages out of my notebook and showed him how to fold the paper into little dogs and then draw their faces. His little figures hardly resembled dogs, but he lined them up so they could see out the window. He tapped the glass for me to look— the little paper pups were watching the real dogs outside going for their morning walks.

Later, there came another tap on the window. It was Dad, outside. Time to go.

Bye, Brooklyn.

2

"Are you excited, Siena?" Mom asked. I could see her hopeful eyes trying to catch mine in the rearview mirror.

"I guess so." I turned to look out the window. We'd be out of the city soon.

Lucca sat next to me, playing with action figures on the edge of his booster seat. Mom took the opportunity to blast kiddy tunes and sing along really loud, trying to get him to open up and sing along, too. But as usual, even though he kicked his feet to the music, he was silent. And the kiddy tunes were annoying. I put my headphones back on to drown them out.

I wasn't sad about leaving Brooklyn. I'd liked my elementary school okay, but not the past two years of middle school. The kids seemed rough and swore all the time, as if it made you cool. But I knew that swearing all the time means you really *don't* know when to use those words. Like when your English teacher assigns homework. That's not really a time to swear at her. Isn't giving homework what teachers are supposed to do? I never really got along with those kids to begin with, and then things got a little bit worse. Basically, I turned into a big weirdo. Much weirder than kids who moan and groan about homework.

But it was unlikely I'd be any less of a weirdo in Maine.

Mom seemed to be hoping this move would be good for me; in fact, it was one of the reasons we were going. She'd always worried that I didn't have many friends, but when I stopped having Kelsey over for sleepovers, she'd obviously noticed that my having just a best friend had changed to having no friends at all.

"We're moving to your house," she reminded me. "The one from your dream."

I'd told Dad about my recurring dream because he likes to talk about that kind of stuff. He'd included Mom in the conversation. I'd told them about the house's rooms, its layout, its large front door, its porch overlooking the ocean. Mom had said, "As long as this dream isn't scary, we probably don't need to worry." Worry? That was a strange thing to say. Dad and I hadn't been worried.

I kept having the dream but didn't talk about it much anymore. But I guess they both remembered. When Mom and Dad went to house-hunt this past spring, Mom called me at Grandma's to tell me she'd found "my" house.

"It's just like it!" she'd said on the phone that night. "It's amazing! I have a really good feeling about it. Dad and I are putting in an offer. Can I talk to Lucca?"

Putting Lucca on the phone is the world's biggest waste of time, so I'd said, "Sure, oh, here he is." I held the phone up into the air and listened to Mom mumble incoherently like Charlie Brown's mom until she stopped and then I hung up.

• • •

"Siena . . ."

A hand was shaking my knee. My mother was turned around in the front passenger seat, trying to wake me up.

I stretched, stiff from the hours of sitting in the car. I took off my headphones and looked around.

"We're here, sleepy. I didn't want you to miss it."

How could I miss it? Sooner or later I'd see the house for the first time. But I decided not to point that out—Mom says I make too many comments sometimes—and got out of the car.

It *did* look like the house I'd dreamed: big, wonderful, an old Victorian near the ocean. I walked across the front lawn, my feet knowing exactly where they liked to fall already. It was eerily like coming home, even though I hadn't been here before.

"It's a bit run-down." Dad followed me, watching me look at the house. He seemed almost nervous, maybe wondering if I'd like it. "But with some fixing up it'll be totally awesome."

I thought it was totally awesome already, but I wasn't about to tell my parents that. I ran my hand along the banister of the porch steps, peeling paint sticking to my hand. It was gray-blue, but for some reason, I felt like it was supposed to be white. Like I remembered it being white. Maybe it was just hard to see the colors, in the dream.

Lucca tromped up the steps behind me, carefully holding on to the railing.

"Come on, buddy, let's explore."

Lucca and I ran all over the downstairs—four rooms and a bathroom with no tub—and all over the upstairs—also four rooms plus a full bathroom that was ten times the size of our old one.

My memories of the house I'd dreamed felt hazy, and I couldn't tell if the layout was exactly the same.

But it did seem similar, I was sure of that. I hoped it was a good thing. Maybe I'd dreamed it because it would be a good place for us. Because we were meant to be here.

I followed Lucca out onto the porch to look at the water and remembered the next part of the dream, because it happened then, too: the feeling of goose bumps rising on my arms. I tried to shake them away. It was warm out, after all.

Dad was carrying things in from the car.

"You always said we couldn't afford a big house." Something I had always wanted.

"In Brooklyn we couldn't. Plus we got a good deal on this one since it needs so much work. Why don't you head upstairs and find your bedroom? Yours is the one with the window seat. Mom and I thought you'd like to read there."

I ran back upstairs to look again. The room with the

window seat was nice. Way bigger than my old room. I stood and looked out the window for a few minutes. I could see the ocean, though I couldn't hear it. And there were grass and trees between here and the water. Grass! And trees! My own grass and trees!

As I leaned on the window seat, staring out at the water, a cool breeze grazed my neck from behind. I rubbed it. Then it felt less like a breeze and more like that sense of someone watching you when you aren't expecting it.

I turned around. I seemed to be alone in my room. There was no furniture yet to hide behind, so where would someone be? Even the closet was open and empty.

I jumped about a mile when Lucca showed up behind me.

"Whoa! Hi, buddy," I said. "Do you like our new house?"

The doctor said it's important to keep asking him questions, even if we don't think he's going to answer. One day, he might.

Lucca nodded.

"Good," I said.

I should have asked, "*How* do you like our new house?" but then I probably would have gotten no answer at all.

After unpacking the car, Dad drove (drove!) to the grocery store. In Brooklyn I'd always had to help carry groceries home on foot. Dad came back with about ten bags of groceries to get us started. I unloaded everything into the fridge or the pantry, while Mom dug through the boxes the movers were bringing into the kitchen.

Mom seemed to think she needed to talk to me before

I disappeared without a lecture, which had been my plan. She didn't even look up from her boxes when she said, "I know you want to explore the beach on your own—and that's okay. Take your phone with you. Never go swimming alone and never talk to strangers, except families with kids."

Bet that was important to her, that I knew it was okay to talk to other kids.

"Can I go now?" I asked, hoping her distraction would be to my advantage.

Dad walked into the kitchen with Lucca trailing behind him, and Mom yelled, "Beds! We cannot sleep tonight without beds! Go upstairs and make sure the movers get all the beds in the right places!" Dad left without a word and I took the opportunity to do the same, slipping out the back door.

From our side yard, long wooden stairs led to a wooden sidewalk that passed through some tall grass and dunes out to the beach.

As I headed down the steps, a sense of independence surged through me equal to when I started taking the public bus on my own.

The late sunset meant that even though we'd been in the car for hours and hours, the beach was still hot and bright with sunshine. I took off my sneakers and socks. The sand felt damp and cool. The tide must have been going out. I walked a ways and then sat down to stare at the crashing waves, to listen to them.

After a while, two kids came along, a boy a few years older than me and a little girl who was about eight. They must have been brother and sister.

They didn't look at me. Should I call out and say hi? But maybe they'd want to talk to me more than just saying hi, maybe even ask me to join them. My voice caught in my throat. I decided just to watch and see if they seemed nice.

The girl's hair hung in wet strings just below her ears. Her bathing suit had a skirt. The boy was wearing swim trunks and looked like he played sports.

"How come you can play with me today?" the girl asked. "Where's William?"

"He can't come over today," the boy said, his tone a bit heavy. "What about you, where's that awful friend of yours?"

"Who?"

"Jezzie."

"You mean our *cousin*?"

"Yeah."

"She can't play today, either." The girl trailed her toes through the water, making deep grooves in the sand that turned into soft ridges as the water washed over them and back again. "She had to go to the doctor."

"Her ears again?"

"I guess so." The girl crouched down to pat her hands gently over the smooth sand. Then she stood up. "But this is her bathing suit. It's mine now. Hand-me-down so

Mama wouldn't have to buy me a new one. Why did you call her *awful*?"

"She just . . . she's strange."

The girl shrugged. "What should we play?"

"Big slimy sea monster."

"How do you play that?"

"Like this!" The boy jumped into the water and stood up with seaweed stuck to his hair and arms. Then he took a big scoop of mud, slathered it across his chest, and howled in a monster voice, *"Arrgh! I'm gonna get youuuu!"*

The girl shrieked and ran, but the boy caught up with her and dragged her back to the water. She kept shrieking, but she was laughing, too. Her brother swung her through the waves and she screamed with happiness, until it seemed like she could no longer breathe. The boy set her down and they started chasing each other through the shallow water, splashing as they went. They ran along the beach until I couldn't see them anymore.

They hadn't noticed me at all. Maybe I would have gotten along with them. Maybe I could say hi next time. Maybe.

I sighed, got up, and found my sneakers.

3

They don't tend to like me, other kids. There's something about me they think is very strange. I have to admit: they're right.

It's why I'd wanted to ignore the man on the bench in the park last night.

I've always seen people in odd clothes, which isn't unusual in New York, so I never thought anything of it. But about a year ago Mom had been invited to a playdate for Lucca with her friend's kids at the playground in Washington Square Park, and I went along. When we were getting ready to go home, I was standing in the archway at the end of Fifth Avenue, looking up the street, when it *changed*. The taxis and cars were gone, the modern buildings. . . . There were horses and buggies, and people dressed in gray and black and brown suits and dresses.

I'd swayed and closed my eyes, hoping that when I opened them, everything would be back to normal.

15

"Are you all right?" Mom was asking.

I looked at Lucca in his stroller; he was swinging his feet as if nothing odd had happened at all. Mom wouldn't have believed or listened to my answer, so I didn't say anything, and she decided I was faint with hunger and pulled us into a little shop for open-faced sandwiches.

I tried to forget the whole thing, but then it happened again. Only it was worse. Because I was with kids from school.

We'd gone on a field trip to the Natural History Museum on the Upper West Side. We went on a school bus and rode in the big semicircle loop where they have school-group drop-off. After we got off the bus, we stood around for a few minutes before they let us inside. We got a glimpse of the pretty park surrounding the museum and of the elevated train that ran up and down the next avenue.

The trouble was, when we were inside the museum and our guide was talking about the beautiful mosaics they'd put in the many levels of underground subway platforms for the museum stop, I raised my hand. "But the subway is aboveground here."

The kids laughed at me. "The subway is *definitely* underground here," someone said.

"But we *saw* it," I insisted. "We saw it before we came inside."

Everybody laughed harder. The tour guide exchanged a brief glance with my teacher. "It's possible, honey," she said to me, "that you once saw an old photograph. The

Ninth Avenue line used to run here along Columbus, on the other side of the museum, but it hasn't been there for, oh . . . more than half a century."

My cheeks burned. The tour guide changed the topic to science. Or, as the museum called it, *natural* history. Things that happened *naturally*. It wasn't natural to have the present fall away and suddenly *see* history, was it?

After eating unnatural chicken tenders shaped like their ancestral dinosaurs, we were given an hour of free time. I sat by myself under the enormous blue whale in the ocean room in the half darkness, listening to its sad calls playing over hidden speakers, my ears still ringing with the kids' laughter.

Kelsey found me and sat down next to me.

"The guide was probably right, you know," she said. "You saw an old photo once before and *imagined* you could still see the train tracks outside. It could have happened to anybody."

"You don't understand," I said. "I *saw* it. I saw a moving train! And I don't know if it could happen to anybody, but it happened to me. You never get it!"

Kelsey looked stung; she had only been trying to help, after all. She wandered off to stare at the fake elephant seals for an awfully long time. On the bus ride home, she didn't sit with me. Nobody did.

Things weren't the same after that. Not with the other kids, or Kelsey, or even just with myself.

Before then, I'd always had these vivid dreams. More

than just about the house. About sinking ships. Plane crashes. Wars. Speeches. I used to wake up and talk about my dreams, thinking they were like everyone else's, and then Mom and Dad would ask how I *knew* about such and such, it'd happened so long ago. I'd say I didn't *know* about it, I'd just *dreamed* it. Sometimes they would catch each other's eyes and then Dad would shrug and say, "Odder coincidences have happened."

But when it started happening during the daytime . . . well, it was just scary. It was scary to be awake and suddenly have the world *change*, to see things that weren't there now. Had I fallen asleep? Or did I really have as little control over my thoughts during the day as when I was sleeping?

• • •

For our first dinner in the new house, we had a picnic of sandwiches on the kitchen floor. I was sure Mom would never let us do that again. She's very into cleanliness, routine, and order. It was well after dark, so it was very late for dinner in July.

I opened my ham sandwich and inspected it. Just mustard, no mayo. Good, Dad had remembered. I put the bread back on and took a bite. It tasted dry and boring and stuck in my throat.

Lucca had opened his, too, and was eating the ham out by itself. After the meat was gone, he started tearing his bread into little squares. Every once in a while he'd eat one.

18

"How was the beach?" Mom asked.

"Oh, good," I said.

"Yeah?" Dad asked. "Wish I'd gotten a chance to get out there. Maybe I will tomorrow, after I swing by the school and see how things look for camp."

Dad's a science teacher and sports coach. This summer he was going to be running a soccer camp. He and Mom had this idea that I should be his assistant a couple of days a week. I'd reminded them that I don't *like* soccer, but Dad said I'd be helping with attendance and equipment more than anything else.

We were all quiet again for a few minutes.

I looked around the kitchen. It wasn't familiar to me from my dream, though most of the house *did* seem similar.

I felt a chill pass through me again. These dreams were really starting to affect me during the day, when I was supposed to be awake and safe from them. I filtered back in my memory through the worst ones. Could any of them come true?

"What if something bad happens to you on an airplane?" I asked.

My parents didn't answer right away.

Then Dad, more used to kids asking questions because of his jobs, spoke first. "You mean like being in a plane crash? It would probably happen so fast that it would be over before you even knew about it. Before you could feel a thing."

Maybe he's right and maybe he isn't. It's not like you can ask people who died in a plane crash if it was quick.

What if the plane dropped suddenly and you got that sickening swoop in your stomach?

Mom took her turn. "Are you worried about terrorists, honey? Statistics show that you're more likely to win the lottery than to die in a terrorist attack."

I almost bought that as comfort. Winning the lottery is rare, so that seemed like good odds. But . . . "I'm not even old enough to *buy* a lottery ticket, so there's *no* chance of me winning the lottery. But if I ride trains and buses and fly in planes and go to public places, then there is *some* chance of being in a terrorist attack."

Lucca didn't say anything. As usual.

My parents didn't really understand what I was asking. I wasn't just talking about what if something went wrong with the jet engines or if your plane was hijacked.

I'm not really afraid of flying. Flying is kind of fun. You get to drink soda and look at the clouds from the top side and, most importantly, that's how we get to Florida to visit Grandma since she moved there. I even flew to visit her without my parents, proudly in charge of Lucca, when Mom and Dad went to go house- and job-hunting in the spring.

And flying is how I'll get to all those faraway places I want to see one day.

What I meant was more about how you go out in the world and continue being you when something terrifying and unexpected could happen.

I decided to try a different route. "Let's say you're in Europe in the nineteen thirties or forties and the Nazis might invade your country any day now. . . . How do you calmly sit on the toilet to go to the bathroom?"

Dad actually put down his sandwich.

"Siena, this is the oddest dinner conversation we have ever had," Mom said, her sandwich hovering an inch from her mouth. "I don't even know what you're talking about anymore."

I sighed.

"Oddest or most odd?" Dad muttered to himself.

"Nobody cares about that right now," Mom snapped at him. "Our thirteen-year-old seems to be having some kind of mental breakdown."

"I am not," I insisted. "I just want to know something."

"I think," Dad said, "that her breakdown is philosophical, not mental."

"Meaning?" Mom asked.

"I think she's trying to . . . pry apart the essence of being in our world."

"It seems to me more like she has some kind of anxiety."

Oh, my favorite. Now they were talking about me as if I weren't there.

"Children might just be more anxious these days than ever before," Dad said.

Mom, Dad, and I all looked at Lucca.

He didn't look anxious. He was carefully stacking those little squares of bread into a tower on his paper plate.

Lucca is three years old, almost four now. There's

nothing wrong with his ears or his mouth or his throat that any doctor can find. He did really well on the intelligence tests they could give him, the ones where he pointed to pictures and played with blocks, so he understood what people said. He just wouldn't talk. The doctor said that sometimes anxiety might make a kid not talk. We don't really know what Lucca has to be anxious about, but that was one reason we moved—Mom and Dad thought maybe he'd be less anxious someplace less hectic and busy.

The other reason was me. The weird dreams, the lack of friends. I'd refused to see a therapist, which Mom suggested over and over. That would only *confirm* that I was crazy: no thanks. I didn't tell them about the daytime visions. I couldn't add that to Mom's worries.

So Dad looked for new jobs someplace quiet.

"Listen." Both of my parents resumed eating but kept their eyes on me. "All I'm trying to say is, this world is crazy."

"You're being too dramatic," Mom said.

"No," Dad countered. "I think she's got it."

4

Mom came by at bedtime.

"You have everything you need?" she asked. "You have sheets, a toothbrush?"

"Yeah, Mom, I'm fine."

She sat down on my bed with me and looked around my room, which was not quite my room yet. "This will be nice for you when it's all set up." She smoothed her hand over my ponytail, and then she pulled out my hair tie and ran her fingers through my loose hair. She had tucked me in this way every night a long time ago, but she hadn't checked on me at bedtime in ages. I liked her fingers in my hair, so I lay down, even though I felt far from sleepy.

"Good night," she said after a few minutes, and she left me alone.

• • •

It was strange going to sleep in the new house.

It seemed extra dark. There were no lights on outside the house at all.

I thought I could hear the ocean, just a little. There were no voices, no cars, no buzzers or elevators or air conditioners. No rumble of the subway underneath. No neighbors stomping around above. There were just the creepy sounds of the old house, of water in the pipes as Mom and Dad used the bathroom before bed, of squeaky hinges as they opened and shut doors, of floorboards. Constant noise used to lull me to sleep; these sounds stood out and kept waking me up.

The salty breeze coming in my window distracted me, too. It was unsteady and somehow damp and cool, despite the warm night air.

Would I still dream of this house now that I was here?

I sat bolt upright in my bed, looking around.

I'd heard someone, I was sure. A voice. Had there been movement in my room?

I must have imagined it.

I dropped back onto my bed, trying to catch my breath.

Then my door actually creaked open, not in my imagination. But it was just Lucca. I guess he was having trouble sleeping in a new place, too.

• • •

The morning was bright, and because there were no curtains or shades on my windows yet, all the bright got right in my eyes and woke me up.

I hadn't dreamed at all.

Lucca seemed to be still asleep, his sandy-haired head on my chest.

I listened to the morning, to birds calling. And because it was early and quiet, the faint sound of the waves still carried up to the house. The air was sweet with all the plants and the water. It didn't smell like pee or garbage or traffic or greasy food cooking, like Brooklyn did. Not that I'd ever left my window open. Air-conditioning was the only choice in the summer. Here, even though it was already starting out to be a pretty warm day, a nice breeze rolled in my window.

I lay there for just a while. Was it the breeze gently lifting the hairs on my arm, making me wish I had blankets to pull over me rather than just a sheet?

Lucca stirred.

"Do you feel that? Like someone's here?"

His head moved up and down against my T-shirt, saying yes.

• • •

"Mom, do you think this house is haunted?" I asked as I headed into the wide, square hallway of our upstairs.

"These are your boxes," she said, gesturing to a stack.

25

"Make them disappear." Then she picked up a misplaced box marked KITCHEN and carried it away.

Had she even heard me? Maybe she couldn't handle the idea of her lunatic daughter sensing ghosts in the house she'd bought so everyone would feel better.

I carried my boxes into my room one at a time. Then I got one of Lucca's and dumped out toys for him on his bedroom floor. His favorites: plastic cars and trucks, Duplo, baby Playmobil. He'd play with them for hours. He always built the most intricate things.

I wanted to set up my collection, but I would need Dad to build shelves first, and he was out at the school. I hung up my posters of places I wanted to see one day: Stonehenge, the Leaning Tower of Pisa, the Colosseum, Machu Picchu.

I opened some of my boxes and hung clothes in the closet. I came across the pink shirt I'd bought with Kelsey—she had a matching one. Why had I even packed it? Why was I hanging it up now? But I did.

• • •

Kelsey used to like my dreams.

The first time we had a sleepover, I went to her house. We'd known each other only a couple of weeks, the first weeks of sixth grade, but they'd felt like long weeks. I'd shown up with a DVD and polka-dot pajamas, and at bedtime in her small apartment we climbed into her twin bed to sleep head to toe.

26

"Siena—you're kicking me—you're kicking me in the face!"

I woke to find Kelsey shaking my feet.

"Huh?"

It took me a minute to realize where I was.

"Bad dream?" Kelsey asked. She turned and crawled to have her head at the same end of the bed as me.

"No, it was okay. I was a pioneer, traveling with a covered wagon. But it was daytime. We got out to walk next to the wagon."

"So you were walking on my face?" Kelsey asked.

"I guess so."

Then she started giggling. And I started giggling. And her mom came by and knocked on the door. Our giggles immediately became silent as we pressed our faces into my pillow.

After we were sure her mother had walked away, Kelsey said, "Tell me more about your dream."

And so I told her about how the prairie stretched on and on as if never-ending, the expanse of sky, the people walking with me who must have been my family. . . .

I realized she was sleeping and drifted off again myself.

• • •

At lunchtime Mom suggested I take my sandwich out on the porch. It was nice out there, with a breeze, and the water was a dull blue, very pretty, that faded into sky in the distance. She also gave me a tall glass of iced tea, which helped me cool down. Then I went to tell her I was going for a walk on the beach, but she said, "Keep going in your room. We'll all feel more free and settled when the house is in order."

She would, maybe.

So while I was itching to get outside and go to the beach again, I ended up stuck sorting my old toys and dolls. I wasn't really sure where they belonged in my new room. I hadn't played with them in years, but I couldn't get rid of them. I left them in their box on the floor of my closet.

The top of the closet had a shelf. If I put the rest of my boxes up there, it would look like I'd finished unpacking. I wouldn't need all my winter clothes out now, anyway. I got a chair from downstairs so I could reach.

When I slid the first cardboard box back, I heard the sound of something metal clattering along the wooden shelf. I shoved the box sideways so I could see what had made the noise. A thin silver cylinder lay along the side wall of the closet.

I pulled it out. It looked like a pen. How long had it been there? The clip of the pen had been engraved to say SEA. That was a weird word to put on a pen. Someone's initials?

I took the pen over to the windowsill where I'd left my notebook, found a fresh page, and tried to write. It didn't work . . . the ink must have dried up.

Mom appeared in my doorway. "Well, there's *some* degree of order around here. Your room looks good. And I found all the cooking utensils, so I can make us a real dinner. How about we all go to the beach together?"

"Sure," I said, setting down the pen. Mom lingered. I walked over to shut the door. "So I can change."

I put on my bathing suit and found Lucca waiting in his at the top of the stairway. I covered him in a thick layer of sunscreen and put a little on myself, too. Mom came out of her room in her bathing suit, carrying our big striped beach towels.

Outside, we headed down the wooden stairway. We walked past the grassy dunes along the sidewalk and came out onto the beach.

"HAAAA!" Lucca screamed, throwing his hands up, and ran across the sand toward the water. He yelled again as he splashed his feet in. A look of shock crossed his face. He retreated and paused, thinking, then let out another yell and went tumbling back in, laughing.

I followed and dipped my toes in.

"It's freezing!" I called to Mom.

"Maine water is very cold." She spread her towel on the sand. "You'll get used to it."

"Why is no one else here?"

"There's public beach parking about a mile and a half away. Probably most people go there. We get a nice stretch to ourselves, isn't that wonderful?"

I set up my towel next to hers. "I'm going to have to sit here and get hot before I can go in. I wonder if those kids will be back today."

"What kids?"

"The kids. The ones who were swimming yesterday."

"I don't remember any kids."

29

"They were really noisy. You could probably hear them all the way up at our house."

Mom was just looking at me, puzzled.

I felt even colder.

I *had* seen them, hadn't I? I mean, they'd really *been* there, hadn't they? I tried to remember what they'd been wearing, if their bathing suits were old-fashioned, but I didn't think so. The girl's had had a skirt, but lots of bathing suits for little girls had skirts.

My heart started thudding so hard my brain hurt. I closed my eyes and rested my head on my knees. I'd only *seen* things before, never heard them.

Just 'cause Mom hadn't noticed them didn't mean they hadn't been there—maybe she'd been inside when I'd seen them. She'd been very busy yesterday. Phew. That was it, no need to panic. My heartbeat steadied and I took a couple of deep breaths.

"Will you help with my sunscreen?" Mom asked, seeming not to notice my brief panic attack. I took the bottle and poured some sunscreen into my hands. As I rubbed the lotion onto her back, we watched Lucca. The waves were gentle and small this afternoon, breaking around his ankles. He seemed so free and happy, running and splashing.

"This seems good for him, doesn't it?" Mom asked.

"Yeah."

I finished with the sunscreen and handed the bottle back. I stretched out and leaned back on my elbows. It was nice here. A lot nicer than summer in Brooklyn.

Suddenly Lucca came running over, crying.

"What's the matter?" Mom asked.

Lucca held out his toes and made a pouty noise.

"Maybe he stepped on something," Mom said.

"Maybe a crab got him."

"Let Mommy look." Mom rinsed some of the sand off his foot with water from a water bottle and inspected it. "Seems okay to me." She patted his back as he stopped crying. "Why don't you get back out there?"

Within minutes, Lucca was playing and splashing again.

"The cold salt water probably helps," Mom said. "If he has a cut, he's not going to be able to feel it too much. But maybe he just stubbed his toe on a rock or something."

When Mom was pregnant with Lucca, I was so excited about having a little brother or sister. And when he came, I loved him. It was fun to watch him discover certain things, but it seemed like he grew very fast, and sometimes I wished he would stay a baby a little longer.

But the way he did stay a baby was one of the most frustrating things about him: he could never tell us what was wrong. He could cry. If you said, "Tell me where it hurts," maybe he would point to a place; if he was thirsty he would go get a plastic cup or open the fridge and point to the juice boxes. But he could never explain his feelings. In that way, we were shut off from each other. I knew loads of things he liked; I loved the feel of his small hand in mine when we walked somewhere; I'd helped him learn to brush his teeth and put on his pajamas . . .

but even still, there was something about Lucca that was unknowable.

Soon it would be even worse. He was growing, and his problem would stand out even more. Would he be able to make friends? Would his teachers think he wasn't smart? Would he be able to tell us what his day at school had been like?

"I can't help but wonder . . . ," Mom started.

The usual conversation. She always started it that way.

Mom seems to think there's some key to why Lucca is the way he is that's her fault. Maybe it was something she ate while she was pregnant with him. Maybe it was something she *didn't* eat. Maybe it was something she fed him or didn't feed him. Maybe she didn't talk to him enough when he was growing inside her. Maybe she talked to him *too much*. Maybe she didn't read him the right books when he was a baby. Maybe, maybe, maybe . . .

"If there was something you did, the doctor would have told you," I reminded her for the millionth time. "He would have been able to say, 'Ah yes, women who eat hamburgers with cheddar cheese while they are pregnant get little boys who won't talk.'"

"Mozzarella."

"What?"

"With my burgers. I like mozzarella cheese."

"Well, whatever, you're not going to guess what happened. It's not your fault."

"How do you know?"

32

"Because I talk. Wouldn't you have accidentally made the same mistake with me?"

"No. That's the thing about accidents."

Hmm. That was true. That was what made them accidents. They were random. Maybe one day choosing mozzarella over cheddar would matter; in a million cases, it wouldn't.

Even though some of her worries seem far-fetched, I think I get Mom the most when we talk like this. Lucca is the one thing that makes her see what I see, about the world being unpredictable and inside out. Things that seem just fine can suddenly change. Like I can't control the things I saw, and I can't fix whatever's wrong with Lucca.

Mom's wrong when she thinks it was her fault, though. It was more likely my fault, for being a bad big sister.

I scrunched my toes in the sand.

The doctors told us that a kid might have selective mutism and be uncomfortable talking in certain situations, like at school. That's not Lucca's problem, because he doesn't talk at home. But they also said that sometimes a kid could be bright, busy observing, and not talk much while he was waiting for his speech abilities to catch up with his big thoughts. In either case, the kid would start talking eventually. Because of this possibility, Dad seems to be a lot less caught up in the whys and whens than Mom and I are.

"I want you to have some more time to be Siena on her

own," Mom said after a while. "Not worry about Lucca. Get out, explore the town. Make some friends."

Lucca was rolling in the sand.

"That's going to be a fun shampoo job," Mom said. Then she turned back to me.

I got up. "I'm going to look around." I didn't want to sit and listen to her telling me I just had to get out there, that making friends would be a piece of cake if I let it happen. How could I explain that the more people knew about me, the less they wanted to know?

I got up and went for a walk, listening for the kids I'd seen and scanning the ground for left-behind things.

When I got back to the part of the beach near our house, Mom and Lucca had gone. I went up to the house and saw that the car was back. I rinsed off in the shower and put on fresh clothes and went to look for Dad.

I found him in his room hanging up pictures.

"Are you busy?" I asked.

"Not at all." Maybe he was being sarcastic, because he seemed to be gently biting his tongue as he concentrated on checking the level, or maybe he didn't even think before he answered me.

"'Cause I need some things," I said.

"Oh?" he asked, lowering one of the frames slightly to the left.

"Yeah . . . *Dad*."

He turned as if just then seeing me. "Sorry, honey. What do you need?" His full attention: that was better.

34

"I want to put up the shelves in my room so I can finish unpacking. And I want some ink for this." I held up the silver SEA pen.

Dad came over, took the pen from me, and studied it. "Where'd you get this?"

"Found it in my closet. But it doesn't write."

Dad disassembled the pen. "It looks like a standard cartridge. Let's head down to the office."

"We have an office?"

"Well, sort of." I followed Dad downstairs to the bigger living room, the one to the left of the front door, to see that the back half of the room was set up with a large desk and some bookshelves stuffed with boxes of supplies. Dad pulled down a box and handed it to me. "This one is full of pens and ink refills. You should be able to find something that fits in there. I'll go take care of those shelves."

He paused in the doorway.

"Did you guys have fun at the beach?"

"Yeah," I answered, a bit surprised by how serious he seemed.

"Did . . . Lucca have fun at the beach?"

"Yeah."

"It seemed good for him?"

"Yeah, Dad, it did."

"Maybe I'll go . . . ask him . . . about it."

Lucca marched into the room then, freshly scrubbed and in his pajamas already, even though we hadn't had dinner yet.

"Hey, buddy," Dad said. "How was the beach?"

Lucca looked thoughtful. He reached up his hands and Dad lifted him. Lucca snuggled against him.

"Come on, you can help me take care of these shelves," Dad told him, carrying him out of the room.

I rummaged through the box, then took the ink cartridge out of the pen and compared it to cartridges until I found one that matched. I loaded the pen.

There was a notepad on the desk, so I scratched out the pen on it, forming big, loopy circles of blue ink. Then I started to write *My name is S.*

Except when I got to the *S*, I didn't write out my own name. I wrote *My name is Sarah Elizabeth Alberdine.*

SEA! I turned the pen in my hand, studying it. What had made me pick these names for these initials? Maybe Sarah and Elizabeth were the first *S* and *E* names I could think of, and they were pretty to write out, but where was Alberdine from? It wasn't something I remembered hearing before.

The funny thing was, I hadn't spent time thinking about any of those names. I'd just moved the pen and that was what had come out, as if something other than my own brain was leading my hand. Or as if it hadn't been my hand.

I took a closer look at the letters on the page. It didn't even look like my handwriting.

The pen fell to the desk with a clunk. I held my hand up and flexed my fingers. There was the little mole, in its usual spot on my ring finger; there was the faint scar across the back from a dog bite when I was three. My hand, definitely.

What was going on?

I shivered, probably from my wet ponytail dripping down my back. I jumped up, pocketed the pen, and went to join Mom in the kitchen, where it was warm and bright.

5

I'm in a boat, but I'm not dressed as a sailor. Dressed for land, I have a heavy pack on my shoulders and a helmet in my hand, ready to go at a moment's notice. The water is choppy and my stomach jolts with each crest. My knees knock together and I wonder, *Am I allowed to feel afraid?*

I can't tell if the men around me—some of them my friends—are nervous. They must be, but some are still talking and laughing as if we aren't in this strange little boat. Some of them have been with me all the way from home—like William crouching next to me, my best friend, in my class since the second grade. We used to go camping. He'd shown me tricks of outdoor survival. It had been a game.

Suddenly we are yelled at to *GO*, to jump out of the boat and run through the choppy water. As I struggle to keep my boots from sinking into the mud, I realize that the water isn't choppy on its own. Men are being hit, falling, around me.

And then it's William hit beside me, William who's disappeared into the reddening water. I turn frantically but am pushed forward.

MOVE! MOVE!

My legs disconnect from the mind inside me, from the heart inside me, and they move, move!

When I woke suddenly, heart pounding, it took me a minute to realize where I was. Lucca was curled up with me again, but I was in my own room—it was just my new room, in Maine.

I rubbed my face, trying to get rid of the aftertaste of the dream, and still had my hands over my face when I got down to the kitchen.

"What, up late partying?" Dad joked. He's been teasing me about teenage behavior since the day I turned thirteen. So far I didn't think I acted like a typical teenager at all.

"Uhh . . . ," I moaned, sitting down in one of our new, high island chairs. "Weird dream."

"Strangely weird?"

"Yeah, I was at war, I think."

"Want to tell me?"

I thought hard, then shook my head. "Nah, it's too fuzzy." I pressed my palms over my eyes. I'd lied: it was vivid, but I didn't want to relive the details.

"You'll forget it soon, then. Here." Dad slid me a plate. "Cheesy eggs."

"These were *your* cheesy eggs," I pointed out as he handed me a clean fork.

Dad shrugged. "I'll make more. What are you up to this morning?"

I scooped up a big bite. Mmm, cheddar and something else. "More exploring."

"Good idea. Just check in at lunch so you can show your mom there's nothing to worry about."

"Deal."

"We're going out to look for a used car for Mom. We'll keep Lucca so you don't have to babysit. But we'll stop in for lunch."

"Where's Mom now?"

"Working."

Mom does writing and editing for journals and books. She's an expert at a very specific thing: the sciences of paint chemistry and art preservation, restoration, and dating. She's definitely more of a scientist, because she has to know a lot about chemical reactions, though she also knows a lot about art history. She does most of her work at home but likes to have alone time to do it.

She came into the kitchen, already dressed and with an empty coffee cup, so she must have been up for a while.

"Morning," she said, running her hand down my pony-tail. "Sleep well?"

"Yeah," I said, catching Dad's eye to tell him not to

worry her with the dream. He turned back to the frying pan and started pushing new eggs toward the center.

"Did you tell her about school?" Mom asked Dad.

He shook his head as I asked, "School? Already?" She certainly was down to business this morning.

"Calm down," Dad said. "I only stopped by to get you enrolled. That's all. You have two months."

I let out the breath I'd been holding.

"We can go see how you like it, though," Dad suggested. "Take a tour, get you familiar with the place."

"No thanks."

"'No thanks,' Siena?" Mom asked incredulously.

I lowered my eyes to my lap, and Dad spoke up quickly, lightly. "That's all right, there's plenty of time."

"Oh, but here, we might as well send it back before the choices are gone." Mom handed me a blue piece of paper. "Eighth-grade electives for first semester. You need to pick one and we'll send the form back to get you signed up."

I scanned the list: Advanced Art, Photography, Newspaper, Beginning French, Drama, and Philosophy.

"I think you should take French," Mom said. "You'd get a great head start for your language next year."

I was actually kind of interested in all those things, but I immediately decided not to take French. "Philosophy." Dad had said my problems were philosophical. Maybe the class would have the answers.

Mom sighed. "Do whatever you want. I guess the elective really doesn't matter that much."

Dad winked at me from behind Mom's back. He was congratulating me on my choice, though Mom didn't need to know about it.

I finished up my eggs.

• • •

After breakfast, I headed out to the beach by myself.

A few scattered houses perched above the rocks. Were they for year-round people like we were going to be, or just for summer people? Maybe it was the steep cliffs that kept this stretch of beach from being filled up with houses.

I found plenty of shells and sand dollars. Left behind by the ocean? Then I found a little shell that a creature had surely lived in recently. That was definitely abandoned. I pocketed it.

I could start another collection, of shells and smooth glass and stones. Maybe Lucca would like to do that with me.

I already had a bucket and shovel in my collection from a different beach, so I held on to any sand toys I found to give Lucca. Maybe we could build sand castles together. The shells and stones we collected could be decorations.

That sounded so fun maybe I was the one who was three.

Besides shovels and shells, I found:

A charm bracelet with two charms—a pair of ballet shoes and a poodle puppy.

A quarter and two dimes.

An adult-size water shoe with a rubber gripper bottom and mesh top. Had it been dropped as someone walked along? Or maybe someone had trouble in the ocean and her shoe washed up on the shore.

That made me shudder.

Why was finding a shoe different from finding a bracelet?

Maybe it's just harder to imagine someone leaving behind a shoe. A bracelet could easily fall off.

But maybe the person had other shoes. Probably she'd been holding lots of stuff, like a towel and clothes, and had dropped it.

• • •

The car wasn't there when I got home.

I set my new finds on the porch. They would have to be rinsed off before I brought them into the house. Wouldn't want Mom getting on my case about collecting super-sandy things.

We were also supposed to brush the sand off our feet before going inside, so I rubbed my flip-flops on the thick, scratchy doormat whose straw bristles reminded me of a broom. It was okay to go inside with your shoes on after you'd brushed them off. In Brooklyn we never wore our shoes inside. Shoes get too dirty in the city. We lined them up by the door. Here, the dirt felt different—*clean*. Whole-some . . . as long as you didn't track in extra. Plus the floors in the old house could give you splinters, so it was safer to have shoes on.

Another difference: it seemed to be okay to leave the house unlocked. The door had been left open for me.

I stood just inside the doorway, frozen. My family wasn't home, and yet . . . it felt like someone might be there.

"Hello?" I called.

I listened closely, my heart beating hard. No answer.

Make a lot of noise. Keep busy.

I loudly stomped to the kitchen, opened the fridge, found what I needed to make a sandwich, and put every-thing on the counter.

I was sitting at the table eating when Mom and Lucca came back with several grocery bags.

"Where's Dad?"

"He just dropped us off. He wanted to double-check everything for when the kids come. Can't run soccer camp without soccer balls. Here, take care of this melty ice cream." Mom slid a container and a spoon over to me.

"No prob," I said, popping off the lid and swirling the spoon around the edges of the ice cream—black raspberry, my favorite. All that melted stuff isn't the same after it re-freezes, so we always enjoy a taste of ice cream right when we get it home.

"Did you find a car?"

"I think we did. We'll get it real soon."

After the melted edges were gone, I put the ice cream in the freezer and went back to my sandwich. Lucca was taking fruit out of one of the bags and placing it gently, carefully, in a pyramid in a big bowl. Mom was unpacking everything else into the fridge.

"Mom, you don't think this house is haunted?"

"No, I don't."

"Lucca knows what I'm talking about, don't you, Lucca?"

Lucca nodded sincerely.

"Are you putting ideas in his head?" Mom jumped on me. "Are you making him afraid?"

"No. I can just tell he notices this stuff, too."

"Lucca, what are you noticing?"

Lucca looked at the ceiling and moved his pointer finger in a circle.

"See, Mom?"

"You two must be in cahoots to drive me crazy."

"No cahoots."

"Look, this house is probably filled with stories. It's been around for over a hundred years. Maybe it's not ghosts like you think, but just a sense of the past. Of history. Maybe you should write some stories about our house and see if you feel better."

Mom had no idea how much of a sense of history I had, how sometimes the images just flashed in front of me as if I were really present to see them.

I carried my plate to the sink. "If I just made up

stories about our house, I still wouldn't know what really happened."

"Might not matter. You might just settle your feelings."

Mom didn't know half of my feelings.

• • •

Things had started going wrong with Kelsey way before what happened at the museum.

There was the business with Lucca, of course. How she said I'd become obsessed with him. How I always wanted to stay at my house now instead of going to hers because I never wanted to be away from home too long.

And there was the picking things up. The abandoned things.

"Ew, Siena, that's trash," she said when I crouched on the subway platform and picked up a string of metal bottle caps. "Don't touch it!"

"I don't think it's trash, I think it's a necklace or something." I studied it carefully. Definitely made deliberately.

Kelsey wrinkled her nose as I put the necklace into my backpack. "You don't know who it belonged to!"

And my dreams . . . she never used to mind being woken in the night to talk about them. She'd often even be the one to wake me, to ask what I'd been seeing. But one night I woke up sweating, having just been in a castle under siege.

"Kels?"

"Rmm?"

"Kels!"

"What is it?"

"I dreamed . . . I dreamed that—"

"I'm sleeping. Tell me tomorrow, 'kay?"

I was quiet, trying to still my heart.

In the morning, she didn't ask to hear, and I didn't offer to tell her.

After that, it started to feel like whenever I wanted or needed to talk about something odd that had happened, she tried to brush it off as if it could happen to anyone. But she wasn't really hearing me. She didn't understand. It made me feel like she didn't like me, the real me, anymore, whoever that was.

• • •

"Yoo-hoo!"

I hadn't even noticed the woman until she yelled down to me from her yard above the beach. She was older, dressed in clothes that looked heavy for the heat, and was tending to flowers that grew in her yard along the fence. Her house, like ours, perched above the beach on the rock ledge.

"What?" I yelled back.

"Just saying yoo-hoo!"

"Oh. Uh . . . yoo-hoo."

"What are you doing out there?"

"Wandering, I guess."

"Are you thirsty? I have some iced tea, made this morning."

Hmm. Mom had asked me not to talk to strangers. But what harm could this old lady do? Could she be the front for some bad guys? Putting poison or drugs in the tea?

I doubted it.

"Yeah, I'll come up." I climbed the steep wooden stairs that wound up the rocks between the beach and the two houses.

When I got up there, I could see under the gardening hat that the lady was Asian. She was smiling.

"I love company for tea. Not that I invite everyone up, but you seemed so all-by-yourself."

"It's okay to be by myself." Was it? I paused. Me wanting to be by myself might have something to do with what was wrong with Lucca.

"I like to be by myself, too, sometimes. I'm Mrs. Lang. Well, here, have a seat."

"I'm Siena." I sat down at a gray, weather-worn table.

She shuffled into the house and came back with glasses and a pitcher of iced tea with lemon slices floating in it.

"Where are you staying?" she asked as she filled our glasses.

"I live here," I said. "Well, I do now, anyway. The big gray house down the way. Number 1445."

"Ah, yes. A nice house."

"You know it?"

"Sure. I've lived here twenty-five years. Always wanted to live by the ocean. My children grew up, my husband passed on, so I came here. How about you?"

"Escaping the city. That's the short version, anyway."

"We have time for the long version."

I sipped the iced tea. Not too sweet, not too lemony, not too strong. Also it wasn't from a mix. Real things are nice.

"Okay, well, the short version works for now," Mrs. Lang conceded.

"Do you know anything about my house? About who used to live there?"

"Not really, because mostly it was rented out to vacationers, like the one next to me. Nothing but vacationers, summer after summer. I presume your place was furnished?"

"All the furniture was gone when we moved in. The old owner must have gotten rid of it."

"I'd like to hear some more about *you*. I expect you're more interesting than furniture."

"I hope so." I laughed.

"What do you like to do?"

"Read and write, mostly. I like to learn things, but I didn't like my old school very much. I play with my brother. He's three. I like games."

"Oh, wonderful! You can stop by to play Uno any time you like. It's boring to play Uno by yourself."

"Okay. So what's there to do around here?"

"Oh, lots of things. We have a nice library. There's a town green and on Monday nights in the summer they have concerts and on Saturday morning there's a farmers' market. You can go on boat rides or whale watches. Where are you from?"

"New York. Brooklyn."

"I bet there were lots of things for you to do there."

"Same things. Libraries and concerts and farmers' markets."

"Did you ever go to the Statue of Liberty or the Empire State Building?"

"Once. There were also a lot of museums and shows and good restaurants."

"The good restaurants here are mostly seafood places, but there's an Italian place and a few pizza shops, a diner, and Chinese food. There's also Nielly's."

I finished my tea. Probably Mrs. Lang could talk and talk forever and liked the company, but maybe she needed me to go so she could watch TV or something and she was too polite to tell me.

"Thank you so much for the tea. I should get going."

I stood up and offered my hand for her to shake. Her skin was kind of soft and her handshake was gentle.

"Thanks for stopping by, Siena. Come back anytime and we can play some Uno. And your brother can come, too."

"Okay, thanks," I said. "See you soon."

I slipped off my flip-flops to walk barefoot in the sand now that the sun was less strong and it had cooled.

• • •

The next day, it was pouring. Dad had to go buy soccer balls. Mom wanted to work and then she and Dad would go get her car, so she asked if I'd mind taking care of Lucca for the day. There was no lightning or thunder, so I dressed him in his bathing suit and I put on mine and we went down to the beach to run around in the rain. Mom yelled after us not to go in the water in case it was choppy. I promised we wouldn't. But it was still fun to play in the wet sand and get soaked. Eventually I noticed that Lucca was shivering, so we decided to go home.

"Your lips are blue," I told him. He ran into the bathroom and stood on his stepping stool in front of the mirror to see.

We took showers to get the sand off and put on sweats because we were freezing. Whew, what a change from Brooklyn! Maine was great. We sat in the living room playing Lucca's favorite game, Candy Land. He kept laughing really loud and Mom kept poking her head in and looking pretty happy about it. I guess she thought this place was working—or would work.

That night, Lucca came into my room, but not to snuggle. He took my hand and led me to his own room, and then he just stood there in the middle, waiting for me to notice something.

"What is it?" I asked. "What?"

He didn't answer, but looked all around, especially up at the ceiling.

"It's the ghosts, isn't it?" I asked. "Don't worry. I'll try to get to the bottom of it."

6

The next day, I had a new destination: our town's main drive with all the shops on it. I figured that was where all the restaurants and things were that Mrs. Lang had been talking about.

Dad had told me the streets to take; it was easy to remember. The walk took about twenty-five minutes, which didn't seem bad. We used to walk a lot in Brooklyn. As I got nearer to the center of town, the houses got closer together: large, old houses with tall windows and front porches and full second stories.

First stop: library.

It was so small! Two floors, but in a building the size of a house. Kids' section on the first floor, adults' upstairs. No separate teen section. There were two computers for public use that looked like they were the first computers ever made.

The librarian noticed me right away, me being the only other person there.

"Hi, how can I help you? Do you have a summer reading list?"

"No." Dad hadn't brought one for me, but surely there must be one. "I guess I'll be getting it late. I just moved here. I'd like a library card."

"Oh, of course. You're old enough to get it on your own, but I'll need some kind of proof of your family's address, something with a last name matching yours on it."

"Dad gave me a copy of the paperwork for the water bill and a copy of my school registration."

"Those will do just fine."

She took the papers and entered my information into her own computer, which was a far newer one than the ones for public use.

"If you want to wait a few minutes, I can make the card for you. You can pick out some books and take them home today."

"Thanks."

She disappeared into the room behind her desk.

I started looking on the children's shelves and found some books with stickers that said YA. I picked something out and then I got something for Lucca: a picture book about a lion. Maybe he'd roar along with the story when I read to him.

The woman had the plastic card ready for me, complete with bar code and my name typed on it.

"Your name is beautiful," she said. "So interesting."

"Thank you," I said. Not that I'd picked it out, but it was mine to carry around, after all.

"Just sign here."

I signed the card and she checked out my books and told me they were due back in three weeks. It was hard to believe that would be almost half the summer.

The store next door sold paintings, mostly of rocky shores, boats on the water, and lighthouses, and the shop after that, pottery. Stuff for tourists. I spotted the restaurants Mrs. Lang had mentioned. Nielly's was a shop in an unpainted wooden building. Through the wide, open doorway, I could see produce and shelves of cans and boxes. But there were also tables. It was almost lunchtime.

I walked past the flowers for sale on the porch and went inside. A few people were buying groceries, chatting happily with the checkout people. Only two of the five registers were open. There was a counter and a sign that said, "Hot lunches canceled for summer. See you in the fall!" Near the tables were a salad bar, a deli counter, and magazine racks. A girl my age was sitting at one of the tables reading a magazine.

I hoped she wouldn't notice me looking around like a newcomer, but she hopped up and came over.

"Hey," she said. Was she being friendly or just curious? She wasn't smiling.

I stopped staring at her and remembered she was expecting an answer. "Hi."

"How long are you here for, a week?"

"No."

Now she looked extra interested.

"How long, then?"

"We're staying . . ." I stopped myself from saying "forever." Too dramatic. "We moved in."

"What grade are you in?"

"Eighth."

"Me too. So's Sam." She nodded in the direction of a boy who was bagging up some groceries. "It's his family's store. I'm Morgan."

"I'm Siena."

"That's unusual. Does it mean something?"

"It's a place in Italy."

"What, were you conceived there?"

This problem is a recent development in my life. When kids my age hear I have a place-name, they all want to talk about my conception. I would never ask about *their* conceptions. What, was it everyone's business now? Wasn't everyone conceived somewhere? What's the big deal?

I rank it as part of the immaturity of middle schoolers. Everyone just wants to mention sex all the time, to make themselves seem to know something about it. I don't really care about sex. Though I would prefer it if we didn't have to talk about my *parents* having sex.

Note to self: don't name your kid after a place. It's no fun for them.

When we were younger, people just used to say, "Cool, Italy. Is your family from there?"

The answer to both questions is no.

"My mom researched art there," I said. "She just liked the sound of it for a name. Thought it sounded certain and strong and brave."

"So, are you? Certain and strong and brave?"

Strong or brave? I was even nervous having this conversation. Was I certain? If I had to ask the question, then I guess not.

But that wasn't really this girl's business, either. Whether or not I lived up to the sound of my name.

Sam had noticed us talking and came over.

"Welcome to Nielly's!" he declared in the exuberant voice of a TV announcer, spreading his arms wide. Then he dropped them to hold one out to me. "Sam Nielly, at your service."

Morgan smiled then, for the first time. For Sam, not for me. I looked at Sam as I shook his hand.

"This is Siena," Morgan told him. "She's named to be certain and strong and brave."

"Oh," Sam said. "I was just named third."

"Third?"

"Yeah. I'm the third brother. Michael and Jack were already taken."

"She's not a tourist," Morgan continued. "She moved in."

"Where?" Sam perked up.

"Ocean Drive." I kept our house number to myself. If

these kids didn't like me and found out where I lived, they could come and throw eggs at my house.

"Wow, beachfront property!"

"It's a dump," I said, even though I loved the place.

"Well, in any case, you can't live in this town and live too far from the water," Sam said. "It's just a short walk for me. Which house are you in?"

Maybe people didn't really go around throwing eggs at people's houses, anyway—what did I know? Mom would say I shouldn't be so afraid of people my own age.

I took a deep breath.

"Fourteen forty-five. Do you know it?"

I was hoping they'd have some kind of story about my house, an explanation for the haunted feeling, in exchange for me giving up the number, but they both shook their heads.

"This is your family's shop?" I changed the subject.

"Yep! Mom's over there." He pointed to a woman in a green store apron like Sam's. "Dad grows the produce and Mom runs the shop. We're all expected to help out. My brothers usually go with Dad and I help Mom."

I was listening to Sam, I was, but I couldn't help that a glint of sparkles caught my eye. I looked sideways to see what was glimmering like that. On the ground, caught in the sunlight—just past Morgan's foot—a sparkly butterfly-shaped hair clip. All alone. Abandoned.

I stretched my foot out sideways, set my sneaker on top of the hair clip, and slid my foot back. I reached to pick up the clip.

"What are you doing?" Morgan asked. It must have been odd to have me practically kick her.

"Just picking this up." I showed her the clip. "Is it yours?"

Morgan shook her big tangle of rust-colored curls. The hair ties she used were so fat I should have been able to guess that the butterfly wouldn't have fit into her hair at all.

"Oh, that's mine," Sam said, running a hand through his shaggy bangs.

"Shut up, Sam," she said.

"Are you going to keep it?" he asked me. "You don't really strike me as the hair-butterfly type."

I was tempted, but someone would probably come back looking for such a nice clip.

"No. Is there a lost and found?"

"We keep a box under one of the registers. Mostly gloves left over from winter."

He led me over to the box. It *was* full of gloves and mittens, and also a small coin purse and a large gold earring and two paperback books. Ooh, a whole box of lost things.

Sam, made curious by my long pause to look at the box, gave it a shake. That woke me up and I dropped in the butterfly. Morgan was looking back and forth between us. Sam put the box back under the counter.

"It's kind of special, right?" I asked. "So maybe only someone who asks for it and already knows what it looks like should get to see it. That way not just anyone could take it."

"Yeah, sure, that makes sense."

"If no one comes back for it, could I claim it?"

"I thought you didn't want it," Sam said.

"I don't want to *wear* it," I clarified.

"You're an odd duck," he said.

Uh-oh. Already labeled a weirdo and I'd known these kids for ten minutes. All I had to do was take too much interest in a stupid butterfly hair clip. Why hadn't I been more careful? Things had been going so well, too; maybe I'd have passed for completely normal.

Then Sam said, "I get a break in half an hour. Have lunch with us?"

• • •

I went outside the store and sat on the wide porch steps.

Had that really been an invitation to lunch?

I opened my book and pretended to read, but I kept glancing up to watch the people walking by. Tourists walked slow and looked around a lot from under their sunglasses. They wore bright, clean summer clothes with the names of Maine towns printed on them. The people who lived here, at least as best I could spot them, walked more quickly and confidently and were more likely to be in cut-off jean shorts and worn-looking tank tops.

Being new, I wasn't really a townie *or* a tourist.

Some other kids my age walked by. They looked at me but didn't stop to say hi. I was relieved. I could only take meeting so many new people in a day. I was already nervous enough about lunch.

The half hour slipped by. Should I go back inside? Would they laugh at me if they hadn't really meant to invite me? Was it worth risking?

But I was still sitting there on the porch, so if they saw me they'd think I had at least *hoped* for a real invitation. Maybe sitting there, waiting, hoping, made me look like a loser. Maybe I should just go. Maybe Sam and Morgan were inside, eating already, laughing at me through the windows.

I turned to check. Someone came through the door, but it was only Sam's mom, who started straightening the flowers, peering into the buckets to see whether they had enough water.

A minute later Sam came out, looking around. I snapped my head forward as if I'd been looking down the street and not into the store for him.

"Oh, there you are. I thought maybe you'd left."

"Still here."

"Oh, good. Mom, I'm on my lunch break!" Sam yelled.

"I'm right here!" she yelled back. "You don't need to yell!"

"Sorry!" Sam yelled. He stretched out his hand to me and helped me up. I followed him back inside. Morgan abandoned her magazine and came to join us, looking unsurprised that I was still here.

"How much is lunch?" I asked Sam.

"Nothing. Not for my friends, anyway."

I felt my face flush. Was he really calling me his friend already?

"I should probably pay. Why should your mom have to give us three free lunches?"

"It's fine," Morgan said. "She says she'd rather have us here eating than out making trouble where she can't keep an eye on us."

"Plus, she'd have to feed us all anyway if we ate at my house, so it's no big deal," Sam said. "Her only rule is we can't eat all day. I have to take a designated lunch break."

Sam handed me a green lunch tray while Morgan got her own. "You can take anything from the prepared foods, the fresh fruit, or snack stuff like chips. And you can go behind the deli counter to make a sandwich, but you have to put on gloves. We make the sandwiches for regular customers, but if you're with me, you're staff."

"Okay." It sounded fun to make my own sandwich. I put on gloves and made a fresh turkey on wheat, then grabbed a bag of chips. I filled up a plastic cup with water and joined Sam and Morgan at a table.

"Thanks," I said to Sam, setting down my tray and sitting next to Morgan.

Sam examined my sandwich. "Looks good. Maybe I should hire you to make mine from now on." Sam had peanut butter with grape jelly oozing out around the edges. Very sloppy. Where'd he get peanut butter and jelly? Morgan had a salad and had also found somewhere to get a heaping bowl of pudding. Obviously there was a lot of exploring to do here.

"The lettuce on your sandwich—that's from Dad's garden."

"Neat." I chewed carefully. My stomach felt funny about the prospect of digesting something Sam's family had grown. Ew, how personal.

"Did you get your tracking yet?"

"My tracking?"

"Yeah, which group you'll take classes with at school."

"Oh, no, I didn't."

"We won't know if we'll have anything together, then," Sam explained. "Did you pick your elective? That's outside tracking."

"Oh, yeah, I picked Philosophy."

"I thought about taking that, but I didn't want to be with all those girls with black nail polish."

I held my sandwich still in front of my face, the polish on my own nails dark against the tan bread.

"Oh. You're one of them."

"Not quite. It's really dark purple."

"Sure," Sam said skeptically.

"Midnight Lilac, actually."

"I like it," Morgan said. "I'll have to borrow it. Maybe then Sam will notice my nails, too."

I didn't know what the deal was between Sam and Morgan, so I tried to steer the conversation back. "Which electives did you guys pick?"

"Photography," Morgan answered, picking up her spoon. "We both did. I don't know, Sam. There might be girls with black nail polish there, too."

Sam answered by "accidentally" squeezing a gob of peanut butter at Morgan. It plopped on top of her chocolate pudding.

"Oh, sorry, let me get that." Sam reached across with a spoon, taking a heap of pudding along with the peanut butter. He grinned while he ate, scanning our faces to see if we looked grossed out. I did my best not to look bothered.

"Do you like it here?" Morgan asked me, ignoring Sam.

"So far."

• • •

When I got home, Lucca was playing on the floor in the living room.

Lucca's named for an Italian city, too. Mom thought it sounded shining and bright. I'm not sure if he lives up to his name yet, either.

"Hey, kid," I said.

Lucca held his hands above his head and moved them in circles.

"Again?"

He nodded. I nodded back to show him I was still on it.

"I brought you this." I pulled the lion book out of my tote bag.

He looked at the book for a minute without touching it. Once he'd studied the picture, I guessed he approved of it, because he grabbed the book and climbed onto the couch, lying down on his stomach and looking through the pages. He wasn't extending an invitation for me to read to him right now.

I headed into the kitchen.

"How was your day, honey?" Mom came over to hug me.

"Fine."

I knew she would want to hear about Sam and Morgan, which made me not want to tell her. But better now than having her find out later and think I hid them for a reason like they're troublemakers or something.

"I met some kids in town."

"Oh? Nice kids?"

"Yeah."

"That's great!" She beamed at me, then pulled me in for an even tighter hug.

I pulled away. "I'm going to Mrs. Lang's."

"Who's that?"

"The old lady who lives next down the beach."

Mom gave me raised eyebrows, and then thought better of it. She was probably thinking, *Why would you hang out with an old lady now that you've met people your age?* And then changed her mind to *Well, okay, I won't bash your choice of friends, I'm just glad you're interested in talking to someone.*

I headed out and down the beach.

"Hello, Siena!" Mrs. Lang opened her screen door when I knocked.

"Hey."

"What have you been up to?"

"I walked into town. Went to Nielly's."

"Oh, wonderful! Did you like it?"

I nodded. She smiled back at me.

"Today's beverage is lemonade in summer citrus glasses." I followed her inside and she set out special glasses with lemons and limes and oranges on them. She got the Uno cards from a drawer in the hallway. We sat down at her kitchen table. I shuffled the cards and dealt and she got to go first.

She put down a red card, and I had one, luckily.

"Are you sure you don't know more about my house?" I asked. "Something weird's going on there."

"What do you mean, weird?"

"I just feel like there's something from a long time ago that was . . . unfinished, or incomplete, or something. Kind of like ghosts. Not too spooky or scary, just . . . a feeling. A feeling that kids feel, not grown-ups."

Mrs. Lang put her next card down. "No ghost stories that I know of. And nothing strange has happened while I've lived here."

I lowered my eyes to search my cards before having to draw new ones.

"Oh, you're disappointed!" she said. "Let me ask my friend Ella Mae. She's lived here forever. Maybe she'll remember something from before I moved in."

We played three games of Uno—she won all of them—and then I had to go.

"I'm glad you were able to come by," Mrs. Lang said at the door. "Come again soon."

"I will. Thank you for the lemonade." Maybe she'd have some information for me next time. Clues, at least. I felt a small pang of guilt; she'd enjoyed the visit just for the company and I'd wanted something else out of it.

It was funny how I felt much more comfortable with her than I had with the kids my own age. That probably meant we did have some sort of friendship.

As I walked home I wondered if the brother and sister I'd seen on the beach had been tourists and since gone home. But why would they have been way down on this part of the beach?

7

I got home just as Dad was taking the chicken off the grill. As we all sat down inside, Mom asked, "How was your first day of camp?"

"Fine. The kids were pretty rambunctious. Want to come tomorrow, Siena?"

"Maybe."

"How was *your* day?" he asked me. "Mom says you met some kids."

Of course she would have told him first thing. She must have been ecstatic—we hadn't even been here a week and already her plans for me were apparently working.

"Yeah. Sam and Morgan. At Nielly's."

"Boys or girls?"

"One of each."

"Which is which?"

"Sam's the boy."

Mom was looking at us like this was an odd conversation. Dad said, "I met two girls today called Mack and Jack. Short for MacKenzie and Jacqueline." He put a piece of chicken on my plate as Mom started serving salad. I took the macaroni and cheese bowl and scooped some out for me and Lucca. I plopped his in a big circle on his plate and squirted ketchup on it to make eyes and a mouth: a smiley face, the way he likes his mac and cheese.

• • •

After it got dark out, it suddenly felt like there was nothing to do. Lucca was sleeping, and Mom and Dad were watching TV in their room. I sat in my window seat with my library book for a few minutes, but couldn't get into it. I kept feeling the hairs on my neck standing up; I'd look around and forget about the book. I ended up staring out at the dark water, lit only by the stars and moon. I'd never spent much time looking at the night sky back in the city. The stars faded behind the city's own lights as if they didn't even exist.

Mom had suggested writing stories about our house to settle my feelings. But making things up wouldn't solve anything. She didn't understand that this problem was *real*.

Then I remembered the sensation of my hand being guided across the paper to write something unexpected. Goose bumps formed on my arms.

I walked over to the shelves Dad had put up, where I'd arranged my collection and set the pen the other night. I turned it over, studying it.

SEA: *Sarah Elizabeth Alberdine*. Who was that? Was it someone real, someone trying to talk to me?

Was that possible? How would that *work*?

Maybe if I used the pen again, I could write something else. That strange feeling of not being connected to what was being written . . . I shivered, remembering.

But this might be the way to learn something. It was the best option I had, at least.

I found a fresh notebook and went back to sit in the window seat, the notebook on my knees. I tried to clear my mind.

I wrote.

And read:

The morning light came in my window as I woke up.

The light was fresh and clear, the beautiful sunshine of a summer morning. I was in my bed, not in the window seat, and it was time to get up for the day. The birds were up already, I could hear them.

But it was nighttime!

I shook my head and the darkness outside became apparent once more. I was back in the window seat, and the stillness of the night had returned, except for the gentle rushing of the waves.

I struggled to breathe. I put my head down on the notebook.

This wasn't normal. It just wasn't.

But I needed to be brave if I was ever going to figure this out. What had happened at our house, why we were here, what it really meant.

I lifted my head.

What if the past was something I could decide to see, when I wanted to?

I'd still be sitting here, holding the pen and notebook, after all. I wasn't really going to go anywhere. At least, I didn't think I was.

I took a steadying breath, picked up the pen, and put it on the paper.

The morning light came in my window as I woke up, shining on my blankets and wallpaper and my dolls sitting on their small bench. The flowers on my blankets and wallpaper are pinks and peaches and creams; they turn pretty in the sunlight.

I climbed out of bed, untwisted my nightgown, and opened my door.

Other people were awake. Vicky came up the stairs, carrying a basket of dried bed linens, just taken down from the line outside.

"I see you've decided to get up. About time."

I would have buried my nose in the basket of sheets

to smell the sunshine on them, to feel their warmth, but I could tell Vicky wouldn't like my nose buried in the sheets she'd just washed and folded.

Vicky doesn't like that I can sleep all morning. She says it's lazy. It's not my fault I stay asleep so long. She won't wake me up because it's not her job, and, because it's summer, no one else is going to be waking me up.

"Your mother's having breakfast."

I went downstairs to the dining room and found Mama reading the morning paper. Without looking up, she said, "You should get dressed before you come to breakfast."

"Good morning, Mama." I sat down, helping myself to toasted French bread, scrambled eggs, and fresh fruit from the serving dishes.

I spread thick gobs of butter on my bread, then spoonfuls of jam, and was on my third piece when Mama again revealed that she was paying attention to me from behind the newspaper: "Eat some eggs and fruit, too."

She folded the paper and set it aside, watching me eat. She kept on the face she'd been wearing to read the news: a frown wrinkled across her forehead. She poured me a glass of juice.

I gulped down a ball of half-chewed bread. "No bacon today?"

"No bacon today. Vicky said we ran out of stamps for it, but she should be able to get some more this week."

I gulped some juice.

"Take smaller bites and eat more carefully," Mama said.

"I'm sorry, Mama. Where's Joshua?"

"Mowing lawns to make a little money."

I sighed. Joshua, usually busy these days. But it would get hot in the afternoon; he'd come home and probably want to go swimming.

"What are you going to do today?" Mama asked.

"I don't know."

"No? I do."

"You do?"

"Yes. Apparently you'll be playing with your cousin. She's been outside all morning."

I laughed. "Really? Why didn't she just come inside?"

"I invited her to, and she said she'd rather stay out there if it's all the same. I said I'd send you along."

Jezzie comes over a lot. She has no brothers or sisters, so my aunt and uncle send her here to be around kids, to play and learn about sharing and things like that. Not that it's done her much good so far. Mostly she comes here to boss me around. My school friends don't live close enough for us to play together much in the summer, so I see an awful lot of Jezzie.

"Are you finished eating?"

"Yes. No, wait." I took one more piece of bread, gooped it up, and stuffed it into my mouth in a few bites.

"Slow down with the bread and butter," Mama said. "Especially the butter."

"Is it like bacon?"

"Yes. We're going to have to get you fake butter."

"Fake butter?"

"Margarine. It comes white and you have to stir the yellow in."

"Really?" I looked at the butter. How could you stir yellow in? "Does it taste the same?"

Mama shrugged: I don't know. "You've had enough to eat. Get along now."

I went right out on the porch, holding a piece of crust Mama hadn't noticed I'd snuck, still in my pajamas.

Jezzie lay on her stomach on the porch swing, rocking it gently with her feet. She's a bit bigger than me. She has long hair that makes me think of that last streak of pink in the sky over the ocean before the sun sets. It's not that color, but that color must be hiding in there somewhere.

"I thought you'd never get up," she said. "We can go pick strawberries next door. Nobody's home and nobody's watching them—I've been keeping an eye out. For heaven's sake, why aren't you dressed yet?"

I shrugged and crunched on the toast. Mm-mm, butter was good!

Jezzie took my free hand, dragged me back upstairs to my room, and found clothes: my short, raspberry-colored dress; white socks; black shoes. She knows my closet and bureau better than I do, she's pawed through them so many times. Luckily, nothing I have fits her, and the only thing she can "borrow" are hair ribbons.

Jezzie does not return the things she "borrows." None of my hair ribbons, and not the black knight she took from Joshua's chess set. Boy, was he mad about that. But he was even madder when the next time they tried to play a game, she insisted on being the white pieces, because who wants to be down a piece? Clever, see, because Jezzie is good at using the knights in chess, too. I handed something to Joshua; he smiled when he saw it, and beat Jezzie using the rocking horse from my dollhouse.

Jezzie helped pull on my clothes and took care of all the buttons, like I was a baby. That's the way she always makes me feel. I let her dress me because there's no getting in Jezzie's way.

She paused to press on her ears. Something's wrong in there—she gets infections; they ring and buzz. Mama told me they are very painful to her.

Then Jezzie pulled me down the stairs and out across the yard, and through some trees and bushes until the house was out of sight and we were in someone else's yard.

She pointed to some low plants in rows. "Go ahead. The redder the berries, the better."

We picked small, round strawberries, soft and ripe, and ate as we picked. They were probably the most delicious, sweetest things I'd ever eaten.

"Lordy!" she exclaimed. "Be careful. You have strawberry juice all over your clothes!"

Jezzie didn't let me eat them all, though; she made

sure I was piling handfuls of them into her handkerchief (the red one, so her mother wouldn't ask about the stains) for her to tie up and sneak home for later. I knew she'd eat them all by herself and not give any to me, so I stuffed as many as I could into my mouth.

Jezzie took my sticky hand and dragged me all the way back to my yard. At the water pump she splashed my face, hands, and dress. "Leave me alone," I said. "Stop it!"

"But look what you did. Everyone will know that you've been naughty. Is that what you want?"

My heart thudded; she was right. But neat Jezzie, who had tucked away the bulging handkerchief somewhere, had not a trace of strawberry on her. I let her clean me off. She dropped my arm and pressed on her ears again.

"What if someone sees us cleaning up?" I asked.

"Easy. We'll tell them you got muddy and we had to wash you up. Actually, that's what you should tell them if they ask why you're all wet."

Jezzie smoothed her hair behind her ears. She wasn't wet at all. No one would know that she had ever done something wrong.

I came to as if suddenly waking up from a nap. I blinked and looked around my room, the pen still in my hand.

But I hadn't been sleeping: there was writing in my notebook, in that handwriting that wasn't mine, about Jezzie and strawberries. About what I'd just seen.

I stared at the notebook page, trying to let what had happened sink in. I closed my eyes, opened them again . . . the words were still there.

I'd been inside a story, inside that little girl! I'd just followed what she was doing; I wasn't me at all—I couldn't think or act while I was in her. But I could taste the bread and butter and the delicious strawberries. It hadn't been like writing; it had been like really being there, like being her.

Her body felt different from mine . . . smaller . . . she must have been younger than me. The house was definitely my house, though the furniture and colors were different. But what I saw, was it—or had it ever been—real? Was this the girl whose name came out of the pen that first time, Sarah Elizabeth Alberdine? It had to be, didn't it? And why was the name Jezzie familiar?

But in any case, strawberry picking wasn't the story I'd had in mind. Unless the house was now haunted by the neighbor looking for stolen strawberries.

I let my eyes wander around my room. The wallpaper was thin yellow stripes on white: sunny for vacationers, I figured.

What had the wallpaper been in what I saw? Pink with flowers? Or peaches-and-cream-colored?

If I'd made the story up, that stuff wouldn't matter. But if I had actually been seeing something real . . . the real past . . . maybe I would be able to find that wallpaper.

I stood up and ran my hand over the wall. It felt pretty

hard and smooth, not like a poorly done job of wallpapering over wallpaper.

But there might be somewhere . . . a spot that mattered less than the middle of the biggest wall. Besides, if I was going to peel back the wallpaper and have a look, it would have to be somewhere Mom wouldn't notice and freak out.

The most hidden spot would be behind the door. There was only a small stretch of wall between the door and the closet.

I ran my hand down that small space all the way to the molding along the floor, and, sure enough, it felt a little off, like maybe there were some air bubbles or layers of paper. I crouched down and carefully peeled up the corner.

Aha! There *was* wallpaper underneath. Blue. Arrgh.

I peeled up the next layer.

And there it was.

Pink. With just the edge of a cream-colored curve: a flower?

A series of chills came over me. Maybe the story I'd seen *was* real. Maybe I *could* see into the past just because I wanted to.

I rested my head on my knees and took several deep breaths.

I crawled into bed and hid under the sheet. But pulling a sheet over my head couldn't keep out what was inside it.

8

The hillside slopes steeply out of the sea toward what once must have been a beautiful village. We reach it on foot, finding only a still-smoking ruin, buildings left in half-standing heaps. On most days the sun would have shone brightly here, but the sky looks gray under the lingering clouds and ashes.

Hello! my buddy John calls.

No one's here, I say.

They must have fled, David says.

There's a heavy smell in the air that tells me that many did *not* escape. The smell alone makes me sick, before my mind contemplates what it means. This is so-called "liberation"; these people are "free" now. I hold a cloth over my nose and mouth.

Listen. I stop the boys, whose heavy boots crunch the rubble. *Do you hear that?*

I turn back to find a little girl standing in a doorway.

Hello, I say. *Are you alone?*

She doesn't answer. I'm sure she can't understand me. She starts whimpering again—the noise I heard—and the whimpering becomes crying.

I've never seen her before, but somehow she seems familiar to me. It's her little-girlness. The little girl I knew back home was blond and happy and well, and this creature is dark-haired, her bright pink cheeks streaked with tears, her nose running.

There now, it's all right. I find a chocolate bar in my pocket, half broken off already, but chocolate all the same. I peel back more of the wrapper and extend it to her.

She turns away and wails, leaning on the doorframe. She covers her face with her hands. There's no door on the frame, and I wonder, *Has there ever been?*

I slip past her into the house.

There's her family—grandfather? and mother?—crushed when the back of the house fell in. The little girl must have been huddled under the stairs with the vegetables, maybe put there for safety.

I go back to the doorway, suddenly numb.

Come on, I say. I lift the girl up against my shoulder. She continues crying, frightened of me, of what has happened. Her little body is burning up.

Where are you taking her? David asks.

Somewhere safe.

Good luck finding a place like that, John says, kicking a large piece of rubble.

He feels the girl's forehead.

She won't make it, he whispers. *And you could catch it, too. We all could.*

She will *make it. I'll see to it.*

I hoist the little girl up higher. I hope someone would do it for my sister. Someone should have done it for my friends in the water, for William. And I hope someone would do it for me.

The sun was up and I could hear the birds. Seagulls. My new room was becoming more familiar each time I woke in it, feeling more like home, but waking from this dream was like coming back from a place very far away. My stomach felt queasy.

There was something different about these two dreams. They weren't like my repeated house dream, and they weren't isolated. They were related somehow. Was I having them because I was in the house now? Did they have something to do with Sarah?

Trying to shake off the dream, I remembered the odd events of last night and hurried out of bed in time to catch Dad before work.

I had the SEA pen and a piece of paper in hand.

"Look, Dad," I said, trying to keep my voice steady. "I fixed it."

"Oh, terrific." He collected the crumbs of his blueberry muffin on his fingers.

"Want to try it out?"

"I trust you that it writes."

"No, really. Try it out." I put the paper next to him on the kitchen island and held the pen out to him.

Dad brushed his hands off on his shorts and took the pen. First he made some loops and then he wrote his name a couple of times.

"Yeah, that works just fine. Good job."

Nothing had happened when he used the pen. So it wasn't just the pen making me see things. The pen helped me, but it wouldn't if I didn't already have . . . well, whatever it was that made me see things.

But at least with the pen, I could decide when I wanted to see things and when I didn't. That would be an improvement. I took it back from Dad. I couldn't lose it.

I was craving something for breakfast that I could cover with butter. I looked in the fridge and found a package of ready-to-bake rolls. I preheated the oven.

"Mom's going to love that," Dad said. "The oven on when we're due for a hot day."

"Oh well," I said.

Dad left for work. When the rolls were ready, I sat with a whole plate of them and a container of butter.

Lucca came into the kitchen, looking sleepy but curious about the good smell. He stood next to me and tugged on my pajama shorts. I handed him a round, hot roll and he started eating.

"I've tried a couple things but so far haven't figured out what happened here. I'm working on it, though."

Lucca acknowledged me by taking a huge bite and smiling with his mouth full.

I was glad Lucca was up early, being his sweet, friendly self. It made the queasy feeling in my stomach subside, and suddenly the doughy rolls and melting butter tasted better.

Mom came in with play clothes for Lucca and started dressing him as best she could despite the fact that at least one of his hands was constantly pressing a roll to his mouth.

"We're heading out the door, honey," Mom told me, sounding pretty anxious. "We're going to playgroup."

Mom had already found a playgroup? She really did get down to things, didn't she?

She knelt in front of Lucca to Velcro his sandals. "Maybe you can tell the other kids your name? I'm Lucca. Loo-ka? Loo-ka?" She pronounced it carefully for him, hoping he would repeat it, but Lucca just stared at her.

I rolled my eyes as she got up, and decided to encourage Lucca in my own way. I held out my palm for a goodbye high-five and pulled him in close. "It'll be fun, I promise." I kissed his temple and he squirmed to be let go. He ran out the door after Mom.

I headed back upstairs with the pen. I was going to try again.

It was Sunday and Dad told Joshua that he couldn't go round asking the neighbors to give him work for money even if their lawns were ten feet tall. Which meant that after church Joshua had nowhere to go and instead went out on our front porch and took apart our radio.

"Why would you take apart a perfectly good radio?" I asked, drooping over the side of the swing in the heat.

"Well, it wasn't perfectly good." Joshua lined up the parts neatly in the cardboard box lid he'd set out so nothing would fall through the cracks in the porch. "I figured we could either spend money on a new radio or I could just see if I could fix it first. It was staticky all the time, so I thought maybe it was dusty inside."

That sounded smart. "Static sounds like dust. If dust had a sound, it would be static."

Joshua was quiet for a minute; then he said, "Dust could also make this sound: shhh shhh shhh. Or no sound at all."

I lay on my back and repeated, "No sound at all."

I closed my eyes but did not hear dust; I heard waves and bugs and the small clinky noises of the parts of the radio as Joshua cleaned them and began to put them back together.

"Should we sing a song?" I asked.

"Nah, too noisy."

"What's wrong with being noisy?" He was fixing our radio, after all. Someone who didn't like noise shouldn't have a radio.

Joshua didn't answer. I sat up to look at him and saw him gazing over the porch railing, out to the end of the water. 'Cept the water doesn't have an end that you can see, it's so far away.

84

"Joshie?" I don't call him that much anymore; that was my name for him when I was little and Joshua was hard to say. "Joshie?"

"What, Little Bug?" he asked, coming back from wherever he'd gone in his head and choosing another piece to put back in his radio. Little Bug was his name for me.

I fell back onto the swing again. "Wanna play with me after you fix the radio?"

"Yeah, okay. What do you want to play?"

"Treasure Hunt." That's one of our favorite games. . . . We take turns taking something from the house, something that won't get hurt outside, and hiding it on the beach, and then we play treasure hunt to find it. The only rules are you can't hide something where the waves will come in and you can't bury something deep, if you do bury it.

"You go first," Joshua said. "You can get ready while I finish this up."

I went inside and drew the treasure map of the beach and yard, selected my own metal cup as the treasure, and went outside to leave it for him to find.

I returned twenty minutes later and handed him the map.

"Oh, thanks," he said, not seeming to quite remember why I was handing him a piece of paper. The radio wasn't put back together yet. He'd just been sitting.

"Come on. Go find my treasure."

"Nah." He sat down on the step and I sat next to him. "You know what I'd like to do?" he asked finally.

85

"No." I'd gone through all that trouble to get the game ready. Now he wasn't even going to play?

"Go dancing. There's a dance tonight at the community center. Want to come with me?" He suddenly seemed much brighter, like his usual self.

"Do they let kids in?" I asked. "You're old enough, but they might not let me."

"But you'll be with me, so it will be okay. I just want to dance. Dance and dance and not think."

"Let's ask Mama."

At first she wasn't sure whether I should go, but she said okay in the end. She asked how we would pay for it, and Joshua said he'd earned enough money this week to buy two tickets. The money raised by the dance went to buy blankets for troops, so Mama knew it was a good cause. When Joshua went to take a bath, Mama brushed my hair out until it was shiny and soft and helped me put on my navy-blue dress, my special dress for parties. Then she found my wide white hair ribbon, one of the few nice ones left behind by my cousin, and tied it so my hair would be held back from my face a little but still be mostly loose. Oh, would Jezzie be jealous that I went to the dance!

"There, now you look angelic."

"What's that?"

"Like an angel. Let's go downstairs and meet your date."

Joshua took longer than me to get ready, so I waited

in the living room, sitting up on the sofa so I wouldn't get wrinkles or rumples. Dad kept looking at me over his newspaper, and he smiled a couple of times, but he didn't say anything. He didn't interrupt my waiting.

When Joshua finally came downstairs, he was so handsome!

"You look beautiful," he told me. All the sad and worry that had been on his face in the afternoon was gone; he smiled and lowered his arm to me.

"Have fun," Mama said as we walked off the front porch and headed for the summer trolley.

We rode the trolley to the community center and Joshua paid for our tickets at the door. There were no other children my age, but there were kids Joshua's age and up. Everyone seemed to take interest in my being there and asked who the little lady was, even though they'd all seen me a million times at church and the library and school. There was dancing for about an hour and then dinner: chicken with peas and carrots and potatoes with watery gravy. Then they brought around coffee. I tasted the coffee and made a terrible face; the grownups at my table laughed and one of them got me a glass of milk instead. Some lady from the community center stood up and thanked everyone and said that we'd raised enough money to send twenty-three blankets! Joshua got that look on his face just for a moment, but then everyone clapped and the band started playing again and everyone was pulling each other up to dance some more. Joshua *was right; I didn't think of anything else, just how fun it was to be swinging around and swishing my navy-blue dress. It was still a hot night and the back of my neck got sticky under my loose hair, but you could even forget about that when the music was good and your feet were going. Some slower music came on and Joshua stooped to dance with his hands on my waist and my hands on his shoulders. A man from the newspaper with a camera asked if he could take our picture, and we turned to smile for him.*

I pulled out of Sarah's mind, suddenly back in the window-sill, clutching my pen and notebook, stunned.

I'd recognized him, Joshua. He was the boy I'd seen on the beach. Which made Sarah the girl. So that had definitely been a vision.

And I remembered where I'd heard the name Jezzie before.

9

I woke in the morning after a dreamless sleep.

I was disappointed; I'd wanted to have another of those dreams, the war dreams. Sarah's story was taking place during wartime; the rationing and the radio and the fundraising dance made me pretty sure it was the Second World War. Were the dreams of the same war?

Maybe it was best that I hadn't had one of the dreams. I always woke from them feeling kind of sick.

Even though I'd definitely slipped into that summertime sense of days without names or numbers, it had been a couple of days since we'd put the little butterfly hair clip in the lost-and-found box. I could go get it and then come back and see what else I could learn from Sarah.

I got dressed and yelled to Mom that I was walking into town.

"Hey!" Sam said when I entered Nielly's. "Siena?" he

asked, as if checking. I nodded. "Come to do your shopping? Want some strawberries?"

I looked over toward the produce, where a hundred small green cardboard bins held a multitude of bright red berries. A shiver ran down my spine. "No, thank you."

We stood there awkwardly.

"So . . . how can I help you, then?" Sam asked.

"The clip we put in the lost and found . . . is it still here?"

"Oh, that. Let's see." We headed to the box. Sam took it out and shifted the contents around. "Still here."

I looked into his face, which I realized was kind of cute. He had a stretch of summer freckles across his nose and blond sun-streaks in his hair. So he couldn't be spending all his time cooped up in this shop.

"Well, do you want it or not?" Sam asked in response to my staring at him as if I had totally forgotten the reason I'd come to the store. My cheeks flushed pink.

"Uh, yeah, thanks." I held out my hand and he dropped the clip into it. Then he shook his head, puzzled.

Whatever. What did it really matter what Sam thought? I'd known all along I was going to be lousy at this new-friend thing.

"Well, bye," I said, suddenly in a hurry to leave.

"You're kind of mysterious, you know." I turned back. "You show up here out of the blue, no one knows where you came from or why you bothered to come to this summerland to stay . . ."

Oh, that was all. Phew.

"They don't know because they didn't ask," I pointed out.

"Okay, fair enough. So where are you from and what are you doing here?"

"Brooklyn. And looking for a more relaxed life."

"Well, here we are very relaxed." To show how much, he leaned against the register with his elbow, but it slipped. He caught himself. "See?"

I laughed. I didn't want to get too comfortable, though: things were going well, but I might muck them up. "Bye, Sam."

As I went down the front steps, Morgan was coming up.

"Hi. What's up?" she asked.

"Just heading home."

She held up a DVD box and shook it.

"What is it?" I asked.

"Some sci-fi movie Sam left at my house last night. He loves this stuff. He tried to get me to watch it, but I fell asleep."

Did they watch movies by themselves or with other friends? Were they boyfriend and girlfriend? I didn't know her well enough to ask.

Morgan and I stood there for a minute, and then she said, "Well, see ya."

"Yeah, see ya."

When I got to my room, I set the butterfly clip on the shelf with my collection. It was a pretty addition. A very personal item for someone to have lost. Good thing I'd found it.

I lay down on my bed, threw my shoes on the floor, and put my feet up on the wall, feeling sorry for myself.

Either one of them could have invited me to hang out with them today. But why should I have expected that?

I pushed the idea of being friends with Sam or Morgan away and drifted into thoughts of Sarah. When I was in Sarah's mind, I could forget myself completely. I could be inside someone who seemed so normal, someone who had a normal brother and a normal relationship with him. And the story felt like it was going somewhere. I hadn't figured out what had happened here yet, but I still bet that I could, if I kept trying.

I rolled over onto my stomach and got the notebook and pen ready.

I lay outside, in the yard, on my stomach in the grass, reading one of Joshua's comic books that he'd lent me.

Mama hates for me to do that, lie in the grass. It gets stains on my clothes that Vicky has to scrub and scrub to get out. If they come out. The worst is when I get grass stains on my white stockings, but, luckily, in the summer heat I hadn't been told to wear any. I would have to scrub my bare knees in the tub myself.

Jezzie showed up with the newspaper and a scowl on her face.

"What?" I sat up.

She held up the front page and read the headline, " 'Town dances to donate blankets to troops.' "

I recognized the picture. "Hey, that's me! Me and Joshua!" I snatched the paper from her and read the caption. " 'Joshua and Sarah Alberdine at Sunday night's fund-raising dance.' " I looked beautiful!

"What were you doing, going to a dance?"

I shrugged. "Joshua invited me and Mama said it was okay."

"If he needed to take someone from the family, he should have taken me. I'm five years older than you."

"Why would he take you?" Inside, I was tickled. Finally I'd done something that Jezzie was jealous of, that she saw as grown up.

"Forget it." Jezzie sat, crossing her arms over her chest. She shook her head many times and pressed her ears absentmindedly. It was several minutes before she spoke again. "What should we do?"

"You always know what you want to do." I kept my eyes on the comic book. "You think of something."

It was true: Jezzie did always know. If I bothered suggesting anything, she would pooh-pooh it like it was a dumb, baby idea and come up with something else anyway. And it was too hot and sticky to bother bothering.

"You are totally boring, Sarah. You are boring like a tree stump."

"You're boring." I obviously wasn't boring. I'd been out to a grown-up dance and she hadn't.

Jezzie snatched the comic book.

"Give that back! Joshua will be so mad if anything happens to it."

"What's it worth?" she asked. "Maybe . . . I could trade you for the newspaper?"

Suddenly a great noise like crying came from the house. Mama came running outside and headed toward the backyard.

She hadn't even noticed me lying on the lawn.

"Mama?" I got up to run after her, but Jezzie stayed put. It was as if she couldn't even hear Mama at all. That was normal for Jezzie, to not care about someone else being upset.

"Mama!"

I found her sobbing, Vicky holding her.

"What is it?" I asked. "What's the matter?"

Mama wiped her nose on her handkerchief. "You'll know soon enough. Go back to Jezzie."

I stood paralyzed. Vicky caught my eye and nodded at me to leave.

When I got back around to the front yard, Jezzie, the comic book, and the newspaper were gone.

The pen slipped in my sweaty palm and I dropped it. The sinking feeling went all the way through my stomach to my feet.

94

I was starting to get a very bad feeling about those dreams. I couldn't be sure yet, but . . .

Maybe I could get right back there. I tried to calm my pounding heart, take deep breaths, and find Sarah again. I lifted the pen and tried to steady my hand enough to write again.

"Siena! Come down to lunch! *Now!*"

Oh, gosh! How long had Mom been calling? It seemed like I was gone longer and longer every time I got lost in Sarah's story.

I scrambled to my feet, knocking over a half-empty glass I'd left on the floor and catching it before it spilled.

"Coming!" I yelled.

I ran downstairs, but I was unable to get rid of that shaky feeling that something terrible was about to happen.

• • •

"You'll watch him for me? Siena?"

I jumped and looked up at Mom. I'd been staring at Lucca eating his hot dog, meat first and tearing the bun into shreds. I'd started this whole visiting-the-past thing with him in mind, to make sure he was comfortable here, and, while I was learning more and more, it wasn't making anyone feel any better.

My own hot dog was sitting on my plate.

"Siena? You okay?"

"I'm sorry, what, Mom?"

"You'll watch Lucca so I can work?"

"Yeah, of course."

I'd take him to the beach. It would be good to get out in the sun for a little while.

. . .

At bedtime, I couldn't shake the creepy feeling from earlier. It hung heaviest in my room. I wanted to know what happened next to Sarah and her family, but I was so tired. Instead of sitting with the pen and learning more, I shut the notebook in one of my dresser drawers. It didn't really help.

I tossed and turned. It seemed extra dark. I was thinking in circles, about what I'd been seeing in the dreams and what I'd been seeing through Sarah's eyes. I didn't exactly know what to do. I hadn't been scared at night for a long time.

Mom would probably have a heart attack if I went in her room raving about ghosts. She was the last person I could tell about my weird visions. I didn't need to add another worry to the list.

I tiptoed down the hall and pushed open the door to Lucca's room. He seemed to be sound asleep, so I lay down on the floor next to his bed on his neighborhood-map rug. It was brighter here, thanks to his Thomas the Tank Engine night-light.

There was tapping on my head.

"Hi, buddy. I'm just going to rest in here for a while."

Lucca drew his hand back up and settled down again.

I tried to settle down myself by listening to his calm, soft breathing.

10

We finally find our way to the base camp, the little girl still slung, asleep, over my shoulder.

You should drop her off with the refugees.

She's sick, I insist. I carry her to the medics' tent. I sit down inside and shift her in my arms. She's limp, but cooler now, and she stirs.

A medic comes over and checks her pulse. *Have you managed to feed her anything?*

She won't eat. She's had nothing but water.

He lifts her eyelids, shines a light in her nose and mouth.

I'm afraid I don't have a bed for her. Just—just hold her for now. I'll see what I can do for medicine. She is so very small.

I woke up feeling dizzy. In the dim morning light, I came to realize that my face was pressed into a small green lawn next to a little house. Oh, right. Lucca's rug.

I rolled onto my side to see my brother's foot hanging off his bed. I gave it a tug; he giggled and pulled it under his sheet.

I sat up. "Ow, my neck hurts."

"Good morning, Lucca." Mom came into the room. "And . . . Siena? What are you doing in here?"

"Having a sleepover."

She gave me a look that suggested I must have ten heads, shook her own, and told Lucca to get up and go use the bathroom.

Lucca came back in a minute and got right to playing. I climbed onto his bed and watched him push his toy cars around the neighborhood map. Sometimes he made a soft "Vroooom, vroooom." Maybe Lucca had a problem like I did. Maybe he never said anything because he was half here and half in some other time, all the time.

"Lucca, about the ghosts . . . can . . . can you *see* them?"

He shook his head.

"*Hear* them?"

He shook his head again.

That was a relief.

"How do you know they're here, then?"

Lucca seemed to think for a minute. He raised his hand in the air and spun it, and pressed it on his head, his chest. Then he stroked my arm.

"The ghosts touch you?"

Lucca shook his head and pressed on his chest, my chest. He made a face like he was happy, then like he might cry.

"Oh." I understood. "Feelings like that. You *feel* them. That's it? Nothing else?"

He nodded and seemed to relax onto the bed. Then he looked me right in the eyes.

"Well, that's it," I said uncomfortably. "You can get back to playing."

He continued to look at me and made the overhead gesture for ghosts again. Then he pointed to my eyes, my ears, my chest. Asking me if I saw, heard, felt.

"Okay." I lowered my voice, and he lowered his hands. "I can see them. And hear them. Okay?" Then I added, "Don't tell Mom."

Then I started laughing. Like he *would* tell Mom. Like he could.

Lucca didn't think it was funny. He kicked me hard in the shin and ran out of the room.

Suddenly it didn't seem funny to me either.

• • •

Lucca had a pretty good kick. After the ten minutes it took to use the bathroom and get dressed, my shin still hurt, and it was turning purple. I hobbled downstairs and got an ice pack from the freezer.

"What's going on?" Mom asked. "Lucca just tore through here a minute ago, then ran out and threw himself on the couch. He's pouting. Have you been fighting?"

"No. That would be way too normal." I took my ice

pack and went back upstairs as quickly as I could with a throbbing shin.

I headed to my window seat and sat there with my leg stretched out and the ice pack on my shin.

It *would* be nice to have a normal brother-and-sister relationship.

I'd tried to shut out the dreams overnight and it hadn't worked. But I did need to know what happened to Sarah.

I reached for my pen and got out the notebook. I took deep breaths and imagined being Sarah.

But as I set the pen to the paper, I heard Mom calling. "Siena, you have company!"

Company?

Curiosity made me hurry downstairs.

Sam stood at the front door.

"Hey, Siena."

"Uh, hey, Sam." Thank goodness I'd gotten dressed. I'd been sleeping in my underwear and an embarrassing camp T-shirt from when I was eight. It was bad enough I was holding a Cookie Monster ice pack and had a purple shin. "What are you doing here?"

"Well, you described the place so nicely, I had to see for myself."

How had I described the place? Oh, yeah. I'd called it a dump.

My mother, in a burst of excitement over the prospect of me having a friend already, showed up with a pitcher of lemonade and plastic cups. "Why don't you guys sit outside?"

"Ooooookay," I said. "Let's go outside."

We sat down on the porch steps and I poured our drinks.

"It's nice of your mom to make us lemonade," Sam said.

"Don't be too flattered. It's from a mix."

"Still. Makes a guy feel welcome." He watched me place the ice pack back on my leg. "Ouch. What happened?"

"Nothing, really."

We sat in silence for a minute. I was careful to sip my lemonade and not gulp it.

"So, now you've seen the place," I said.

"Yep. Nice place. Not a dump. Probably needs a new roof."

"Yeah, I wouldn't mention that to my parents."

"I'm sure they know already. This *is* a relaxing life," Sam announced, stretching out on the porch.

It seemed like he was making a point to show he had listened to the things I'd said before.

"Let's go in," I said after I'd gotten two mosquito bites. I brought the pitcher back to the kitchen.

Sam didn't make it into the kitchen with me. I backtracked and found that he'd gotten caught in the living room. He was crouched on the floor with Lucca, playing with his train set. Lucca never sets up his tracks in an easy oval or figure eight, but uses track splitters to make elaborate designs all over the floor.

"Look, Thomas trains! I love Thomas trains!" Sam exclaimed. Lucca beamed.

Sam got so absorbed that I sat on the couch, watching. Were Lucca and I still in a fight? It's hard to know with someone who never talks to you.

Mom stuck her head in. "It's lunchtime. Want to stay, Sam?"

"Sure."

Mom told Lucca to wash his hands, and he ran off.

When we were alone, Sam said, "Your brother's shy. He wouldn't even tell me his name."

"His name's Lucca. And he's not shy. He just doesn't talk."

"At all?"

I shook my head.

Sam looked thoughtful. "Why not?"

"Your guess is as good as mine." I hopped off the couch and we went to join Mom and Lucca in the kitchen.

As we ate I kept glancing sideways at Sam, who seemed much more comfortable than I was. He caught me looking at him three times, so I stopped looking.

Why didn't we have any napkins? What if I had mustard on my mouth? Would it be worse to leave it there or to wipe it on the back of my hand?

And why did I suddenly care so much about mustard on my face?

Lucca and Sam started trading broken pretzels for whole pretzels and then built something that looked like a log cabin out of the leftovers.

Mom kept beaming at me, even though I didn't say a word.

• • •

"I have to go to the store," Sam announced once the table was cleaned up. "Thanks for lunch!" he said to Mom.

"Anytime."

"Come on, I'll walk you out," I said, and we walked to the end of the driveway.

"I'll see you soon," he said.

Really? I'd been boring as a box of bricks. But I said, "Yeah, see you soon. Thanks for coming over."

After I came back inside, I spotted Lucca sitting on the toilet in the downstairs bathroom with the door open. His feet were resting on his toddler stepping stool and a picture book sat on his knees.

He couldn't read, so he was looking at it.

Well, maybe he could read, but no one would know, right? Maybe he was a super-genius who should have been reading *War and Peace* already.

"Listen, Lucca," I said, coming into the bathroom and crouching down to be at his eye level. "You're three years old. That's old enough to shut the door when you go to the bathroom." Especially now that people might be dropping by. People who might not understand a three-year-old's bathroom habits.

Lucca's eyes widened at me. I knew what he was thinking.

"Oh, if you need help? Just call us. Bye!" I left the bathroom, Lucca still staring at me as I shut the door.

I headed into the kitchen.

"Mom, I just told Lucca it's time he started going to the bathroom with the door shut."

"What?"

"Yeah, he's getting older, it's ridiculous."

"He's not that old. How will we know if he needs help?" Mom started to leave the room, to go open the bathroom door.

"Wait." I grabbed her arm. "You can always go in to check on him. But this way, maybe he'll call for someone."

Mom paused to consider my point.

"That's tough love, right?" I explained. "Maybe he's uncomfortable, but it could help."

"You aren't his parent, Siena. It's not up to you to decide and enforce the lessons."

"Well, what are *you* doing?" I asked. "Put him in a situation where he really needs to talk, and maybe he will."

Mom looked angry, but then she sighed and spoke calmly. "Upsetting him won't work either. It might even make things worse, rule out the chance of improvement."

The sound of a toilet flushing made us pause. Then it flushed again, and again. Then there was a thunk that sounded like a book being thrown against a wall.

Mom and I forgot that we were in the middle of an argument and started laughing.

"I guess it backfired," I admitted. "He worked out signals."

"I'll go see what he needs."

"About the door? It's just so much more civilized with it shut."

"We'll compromise: I'll have him shut the door except for the last inch . . . no need to risk him getting locked in a bathroom."

"Deal." I headed upstairs to the window seat. The water looked beautiful and a cool breeze blew in through the screen.

I was surprised Mom hadn't given me a lecture about window safety. I know not to lean on the screen, but I'd have to make sure Lucca didn't visit my room and try it.

Oh, Lucca, are you ever going to talk to us?

11

My mind was scattered. Lucca still seemed to be mad at me, and Sam—why had he stopped by? Did he want to be friends after all?

But I needed to get back to Sarah, to finding out what happened, and what I was still sensing here. I picked up the pen.

We were sitting around the dining room table, me, Mama, Dad, and Joshua. Mama still had red, dripping eyes.

Dad looked about as upset as Mama, though he was not crying.

"This was bound to happen sooner or later," Dad said. "Not that it makes it easier to let you go, son, but so many of our boys are being drafted."

"It'll be all right," my brother said. "I'm ready to serve."

Mama buried her face in her handkerchief again.

I kept quiet. I couldn't eat anything.

The silence continued until Joshua said, "May I be excused?"

"Of course, Joshua," Dad said.

After he'd left, I looked up. "Me too?"

I walked upstairs and found him in his room, sorting through some of his belongings.

"Hi, Sarah."

"Are you taking all your things when you go away?"

"Nah. You don't really get to take much."

Suddenly I understood why the boys in the war didn't have enough blankets. That was why we'd had the dance.

I ran over to where he sat on the bed, jumped into his arms, and pressed my head into his chest. "I don't want you to go!"

"I know, Little Bug." He pulled me off him, just far enough so that we could look into each other's eyes. "Can I tell you a secret?"

Ooh, a secret. Those special words that give you a tiny piece of someone else to carry around, to prove you know something important about them.

"Yes. I won't tell. Cross my heart."

"I wasn't drafted, like I told Mom and Dad. I enlisted."

I stared at him.

He realized I didn't know the difference. "Mom and Dad think the government sent a letter saying I had to go. It wasn't like that. I signed up myself."

"Why would you do that? Why would you want to go away?"

"It's not about going away, it's about helping. Half my class has signed up. If I didn't sign up, I would always doubt my own courage. I didn't want to do that. I wanted to show I was ready."

I didn't see why he needed to do any of it. But his eyes told me that it was very important to him.

"I'll keep your secret," I promised.

And then I was back in the present, staring at the words on the page. That was it—it had just stopped. Sarah had no more to tell me right now?

Oh, no. Joshua. Joshua would be going off to war.

No, this story had happened already, in the past.

Joshua *went* to war.

Suddenly I had flashes of churning red water; the bombed, abandoned town; a sick little girl in my arms. They weren't just dreams; they were memories. Joshua's memories. I had seen them in my sleep, without knowing it, just like I'd seen this house and it turned out to exist.

Why was I having Joshua's memories? I felt a little shaky and lay down on the window seat.

Calm down.

Think.

I was getting somewhere in the ghost mystery. Maybe Joshua hadn't made it home? Could his spirit have come all the way back from overseas just to haunt this house? Spirits could probably go anywhere they wanted, in time or space.

Or maybe it was someone else? Maybe his mom had gone a little nuts in his absence and it was her spirit who was here, still waiting for her son to come home?

I'd have to find out later. It was never possible to get right back into Sarah's mind. I sat up and went downstairs to look for company, but there was a note from Mom on the kitchen counter, saying that she and Lucca had gone to playgroup. They'd be back soon.

I scribbled, *At the beach—S* across the bottom of Mom's note and left it on the counter.

On the beach, I sat down in a meditating pose and tried to sense if I felt the spirit-feeling out there. I did, kind of. But only near our own section. I spent ages wandering farther down the beach, where it felt normal: lonely, and windy, but not like I had extra company.

Why was it that Mom and Dad didn't seem to feel the extra presences? Was it just a kid thing—because Sarah the Ghost was a kid? But not Joshua. He went off to war.

By this time, I had wandered down to Mrs. Lang's house. I knocked on her door.

"Hi, Siena!" she greeted me. "I was just sorting some old clothing to give away. But it might be a good time for a break."

She shuffled down the hallway and got the Uno cards. Before she had even dealt them, she said, "I got a chance to visit Ella Mae."

"And?"

"She said that the owner hasn't lived in the house for a long time, over half a century, that the house has mostly been rented out. But before that, back in the forties, when Ella Mae was young, a family lived there. She didn't know them personally, but she knew of them because they were kind of a strange family. There were two children: a boy, who went off to the war and then came back unwell, and a girl, who wouldn't ever talk. The mother and father in turn shut off to most of the world. Rumors spread that the whole family was mentally ill."

My heart started pounding. The boy who'd gone off to war and the girl who was his sister were in my visions—that was scary enough to think of—but it didn't quite match. . . . If what Mrs. Lang was telling me was true, Joshua had made it back and Sarah . . .

"They were all mentally ill? The girl didn't talk?"

"Those were rumors. But there was something about them, something unstable or odd."

I felt sick. Could Sarah be the girl who didn't talk? She talked in my version of the story so far; what had happened?

But wait a minute . . .

Let's say she didn't talk . . . and there was something weird in the family and several of them didn't talk much . . . and we had moved here because Lucca didn't talk . . . that was just . . . all twisted up and scary. Maybe we didn't belong here at all. Maybe we belonged as far from here as possible.

"I have to go!" I said, pushing back from the table and standing up.

"We haven't even started yet," Mrs. Lang said, surprised.

"I'm sorry. . . . I'll come back soon!" I ran out the door and all the way home. The sand under my feet said *Shouldn't, shouldn't.*

We *shouldn't* be here, *shouldn't, shouldn't.*

I found Mom on the porch, using a paint peeler and sandpaper to get the old paint off the railings.

"Why did you pick this house?" I blurted out, not even bothering to catch my breath.

"What?" she asked, startled.

"Why did you pick this house?"

"Repainting isn't going to be so bad, Siena."

"I'm not talking about painting. I don't care about painting. I want to know why we came here—*here*, to *this* house."

Mom seemed to think this was more of my bizarre, over-analyzing behavior. She calmly explained as she continued peeling paint, "We already told you. We looked at a lot of houses. This one reminded us of the one you'd talked about and . . . I don't know, maybe because of that, I liked the feeling here. It just felt right. It felt like something here would help Lucca. Or maybe it was the beach. Something about the beach would help Lucca."

"Something here would help Lucca?"

"Yeah, I think so. Just a feeling I had. Still have, actually."

Her steady voice calmed my thumping heart. But still . . .

"What if it isn't to help him? What if it's a trap . . . what if there's something wrong here?" What if I had dreamed it up for the wrong reasons? For reasons that would hurt us? What if a bad spirit had pulled us here?

"Siena, there's nothing wrong here. You always think there's something wrong *everywhere*. Hey, here . . ." She turned to a box of supplies and fished out another paint scraper. "It might calm you down to help me. Make some improvements. Not think too much about . . . whatever it is."

I took the scraper and began to work on my own section of the railings. She was right, it did calm me down. About twenty minutes later, she asked, "Setting your panic attack aside, do you like it here, Siena? I mean, for *you*?"

"I think it's great here. For me."

"I'm so glad. There was always a chance it would end up being harder for you, starting over."

"No, I like it."

"Your brother—that's hard on you, isn't it?"

I shrugged. "I love Lucca." I felt a squirm of guilt in my stomach. "Maybe I'm not always the *nicest* sister to him." In fact, yesterday I'd been downright horrible.

"Nobody's perfect one hundred percent of the time. Usually you're very good with him."

Mom's so contradictory sometimes. Like she was mad

113

about us fighting yesterday, but now it sounded like not such a big deal.

And she's so funny, too, because sometimes she acts like I'm nutso for worrying about some things and other times she totally gets it.

We both went back to scraping.

Finally I said, "It's just that it's so easy for something to turn out different than you expected." I *had* expected that Lucca and I would get along great, that he would get me in a way my parents didn't. And in a lot of ways he did, but then . . .

"That is kind of scary," Mom said. "But it's also the kind of thing where you get to show how strong you are."

"I'm not, though. I'm all mush inside."

"No. It would be so easy for you to get frustrated with a brother like Lucca, one who needs a lot of extra attention."

"He's just a little boy. I know he needs help. And love." Even if I didn't always show it.

"He does. You are very wise to see that."

I took a deep breath. "I sometimes wonder if he doesn't talk because he doesn't like us."

"You know . . . I wonder that sometimes, too, when I think of the long list of whys; I can't help it. But think of how he sneaks into our beds to cuddle, or how he reaches up to hold our hands, or how he laughs when we play with him. He wouldn't do those things if he didn't like us."

"That's true. Then what is it?" Was it my fault?

"It's a mystery," Mom answered. "But one day, it might just disappear. You just need to hang on and believe it will. That's what I'm doing."

Again, Mom is funny. She tries and she tries and she tries and then she says when it comes down to it, she's just hanging on.

• • •

I was in the kitchen chopping up veggies from the farmers' market when the house phone rang.

"I'll get it!" I yelled. It was kind of exciting to have the phone ring. So far it had only rung twice, when Grandma called.

"Hello?"

"Hi. Is this Siena?"

"Yes."

"It's me. Sam."

"Oh, hi!"

Sam. I don't know who I'd been expecting.

He was so funny: just showed up when he felt like it, just called at dinnertime. Wacko.

"What's up?" I asked.

"Just called to say hi. What are you doing?"

"Helping make dinner." I headed back over to the counter and the cutting board. "How'd you get our number? *I* don't even know this number."

"It was on your fridge. With a note that said 'Learn this number: our new house phone.'"

At first I thought he was joking, but when I turned to look at the fridge, he was absolutely right; the note was there, in Dad's handwriting.

"And you memorized it?"

"Well, I only had to remember the last four digits. The others are the same as everyone else's in town."

"Is that Sam?" Mom asked. "Let me talk to him after."

I gave her a look like *she* had ten heads.

"Just really quick. When you're done."

I nodded at her and turned away.

"What did you do today?" I asked him.

"Morgan and I went tubing."

"You did?"

"Yeah, it was fun! You should come next time."

"Maybe I will." Maybe. If I was actually invited. "Where do you go?"

"There's a good river about twenty minutes away. My uncle drops us off a few miles up and then meets us at the end where the river dumps into the ocean."

"Do you worry about getting pulled out to sea?"

Sam laughed. "No. Should I?"

No, that was me. I was the worrywart, about everything.

"Oh—my mom wants to talk to you."

"She does? What for?"

"No idea."

116

I handed over the phone.

"Hi, Sam. Yes, I'm fine, how are you? I was wondering if you would be interested in coming over to play with Lucca and I'll pay you. It will be kind of like babysitting, except we'll be around most of the time. He seemed to like you and I think having a boy around might be good for him. We could make it a regular thing."

My mouth dropped open. What was she *doing*?

"Yeah, okay . . . so twice a week? That sounds good for us. Okay, see you then."

She hung up.

"*Mom!*"

"What?" she asked innocently.

"You're asking him to work here?"

"Well, not exactly. I'm asking him to play with your brother."

"*Mom!*"

"Chill out. Didn't you think he played nicely with Lucca?"

"Yes, but—"

"And Lucca liked him. There's a chance he'll warm up to him some more. . . ."

"Yes, but—" She had just been talking about how she was waiting out this thing with Lucca. Yeah, right! She did nothing but try to get him to talk!

"And look at it this way." Mom gave me a goofy smile. "I've just ensured he'll be coming back here. So he'll be around to spend more time with you, too."

"That doesn't— You hardly— You didn't even— *Agh!*"
I stormed out of the kitchen.

But . . .

Infuriating as Mom was, it would be nice to have Sam around.

12

In the morning I was pacing in my room, then I paced up and down the stairs, then I paced around and around the circle made by the connecting hallways of the downstairs rooms. I was thinking, thinking. . . . If it was true, what Mrs. Lang had said . . . then it meant . . . No, it didn't. . . . Twice I sat down in the window seat and picked up the pen, but twice the thought of continuing the story, no matter what I could learn, made me put the pen back down and return to pacing.

"You need something to do! Here." Mom thrust twenty dollars and a shopping list at me. "Go into town. Nielly's has great produce."

"I— But—"

"Nope, not listening. Get out of here."

I couldn't even explain that that was Sam's family's place. I wondered if Mom already knew. That would so be like her, to send me there *because* she knew.

119

I found myself pushed onto the front porch, clutching a pair of sneakers I hadn't picked up, with the door shut behind me.

Well, horribly embarrassing as it was, I would have to see him again soon enough anyway. Might as well get it over with.

I groaned and sat down to put the shoes on.

"You didn't give me any socks!" I called at the house.

A minute later the door opened, a pair of socks flew through it, and it slammed shut again.

Maybe Sam wasn't working today.

I trudged into town and up the steps of Nielly's.

Morgan was at a table reading a magazine (didn't she have anything else to do?), and Sam was leaning on his elbow at one of the registers.

"Hi," I said in a dull tone.

"Hi," he replied in the same tone, imitating me.

Then we both stood there. Morgan's magazine clunked against the table as she set it down.

Sam smiled slyly and said, "So, I'm coming to your house tomorrow for a playdate."

I crossed my arms over my chest. "I couldn't believe she asked you to do that. So annoying. I'm really sorry."

"Why? It's totally cool. Easy job. I'll get some more money and then we can go to the movies on the weekend or eat junk at the diner. Maybe your mom will invite me to stay to eat again."

"Again?" Morgan chimed in. "I didn't know you'd eaten there before." She came over.

Sam and I both ignored her interruption.

"It's just a plot, you know," I said. "She wants you to get my brother to talk. Or at least help him socialize."

"Who cares why? That would be pretty cool, wouldn't it? If he started to talk?"

"Yeah."

"So what's the problem?"

I felt my cheeks get hot as I realized the problem: Mom was also trying to help *me* socialize by having Sam come over on a regular basis.

"What are you guys *talking* about?" Morgan asked.

"Nothing. Siena's little brother has no brothers, so I'm going over to play and be like . . . a brother."

He didn't add that Lucca was different.

"You're really okay with it?" I asked.

"Totally. So super, completely, definitely, A-okay."

"Then I guess I am, too."

"Good."

"Is that why you came by?" Sam asked.

"No. This was *also* my mom's idea." I took the shopping list out of my pocket and unfolded it. "Leafy lettuce. Two beefsteak tomatoes. One white or yellow onion."

"Allow me to assist you." Sam bowed and proceeded to the produce section. He paraded about, making a show of selecting vegetables, and then returned to the counter. "Our leafiest lettuce." He held it up and set it gently into a paper bag. "Our two most beautiful, beefy beefsteak tomatoes." He nestled them in next to the lettuce. Then he held up two onions and extended them in turn as he announced, "one white or one yellow onion."

"Uh, yellow, please."

He rang everything up, gave me change, rolled down the top of the paper bag, handed it to me, and said, "See you tomorrow."

• • •

That night as the sun set, I sat in the window, holding the pen. Still afraid to put it to paper. What would I learn about Sarah? What would I learn about *us*?

I set the pen back down and went outside. I found Dad on the front porch and sat next to him on the floorboards.

"We'll have to get some furniture," he said. "So it's nicer to sit out here."

"It's nice out here now, Dad. 'Cept for the mosquitoes." I slapped at one on my elbow and left a bloody smear; she'd gotten me.

The arc of the moon appeared over the water, lighting a path. While we sat there, incredibly, the full moon rose so fast you could see it happen.

"Look at that!" Dad said. "Wish Lucca could see. Not that I'd wake him up. Not tonight, anyway."

I pictured Lucca standing on the porch, saying, "Look at the moon!" I filled in his voice with an imaginary one, one that was a combination of the baby voice we used to hear a long time ago and the toddler voice he uses to yell his happy sounds when he plays.

I took a deep breath. "Dad? Would you do anything for Lucca? Even if it was something hard and maybe scary?"

"What did you have in mind?"

What *did* I have in mind? I wasn't even sure. But I'd been afraid to keep going, to find out. What if there were no answers here, but only questions?

• • •

It was Mom who met Sam at the door at four-thirty the next day, not me. I waved to him from the stairs. He smiled and waved back, while listening to Mom tell him some of the things that Lucca liked to do.

It was weird: Sam was in the house, but not to see me.

I headed back up to my room, where I stared at Sarah's pen.

This whole thing was too creepy.

But something must have happened between what I'd seen and the way the family ended up, because Sarah had talked just fine so far. What was it? What had happened?

I picked up the pen. I could do this. I could find out what happened. I got my notebook, too, sat in the window seat, and tried to quiet my own thoughts, to open my mind.

But as I moved the pen across the paper, I got nothing but loopy scribbles.

Sam stayed for dinner.

"You guys have fun?" Mom asked him and Lucca when they came to the table.

Lucca nodded. Mom beamed at both of them. I made a face into my plate but no one noticed.

"Good," Dad said. "Rice, Sam?"

"Thanks." Sam took the spoon. The rice fell all over his plate instead of in a neat, round heap like I like to make. I looked back at my own plate when he noticed me looking at his.

"How do you like your school, Sam?" Dad asked.

"Fine. I mean, I'm glad it's summer, but . . ."

"No, I get it." Dad laughed. "I'm a teacher. I like the summer, too. Do you feel like you get a lot of homework?"

"Some days are really bad but most days are okay. It depends on your tracking."

"We don't have Siena's tracking yet," Dad said. "Her transcripts from her old school haven't come yet."

Mom made a "tut" of annoyance. Lucca echoed it over and over between eating individual grains of rice with his fingers. There was a general pause at the table while we listened.

"Well, anyway, Siena hasn't gone to see the place yet," Dad said.

"I could show you around," Sam said to me.

"Okay."

"That would be nice," Dad said.

"I thought you weren't interested," Mom teased me, with raised eyebrows.

"Well, maybe I *should* go see it."

Mom caught Dad's eye. "I guess school's more appealing with the right company."

I ignored that. So did Dad.

"I can drop you off there tomorrow on my way to work," Dad said. He looked at Mom.

"I'll pick you up," she said.

I hoped she'd be able to resist going inside herself.

• • •

The school was a low, sprawling brick building, only two stories in the tallest sections. Fields and parking lots surrounded it. It was the opposite of any school I'd ever seen in New York, where the closest thing to fields were paved recess yards and several floors were stacked on top of one another.

"Three towns use this middle school," Sam told me. "About eight hundred kids."

He led the way through the front door. No security. *That* was different.

There was a man walking in the hall. He had a little stubble on his face and he looked kind and happy.

"Hi, Mr. Walker," Sam said. "Siena, this is our principal. This is Siena."

"Hello, Siena, welcome." Mr. Walker shook my hand. "Sam, I'd have thought you'd stay miles away from here all summer."

"I wanted to show Siena around. She's starting in the fall. She just moved here."

Mr. Walker turned back to me. "Lovely to meet you. Take a look around. Glad you wanted to come by. I'd show you myself, but I'm late for a meeting. Sam will do a good job."

We headed on our way. Every few rooms there were teachers having meetings in small groups. When Dad's soccer camp was over, he'd go to plenty of those meetings at his new high school. One hallway had rooms with a couple of classes in session. "Summer school," Sam whispered. I tried to get a look at the kids as we passed by.

Two kids never would have been able to show up and walk around my old school because they felt like it. Just that tiny thing made me feel good. It felt like kids were actually welcome at school, invited. The classrooms were bright and airy and some on the ground floor had extra doors leading right outside.

But mostly, I was enjoying the sound of Sam's voice, and the fact that all his attention was focused on me.

13

Mom refrained from coming inside when she picked us up. She dropped Sam at Nielly's and I went to the library.

I brought a new book home for Lucca, but at bedtime he handed it to Dad. He didn't want me to read to him. He was still mad at me.

I went to my room again and sat looking at the pen. What had been going wrong? Was it just me being afraid? Was I not being open enough to see her story?

Don't be afraid, Siena, I told myself. *Knowing can't hurt you.*

I got the pen and notebook and sat in the window seat.

I just had to let go. Of Lucca being mad. Of thoughts of Sam and school. Of everything. To just be open to Sarah.

I put the pen to the page, closed my eyes, and drifted.

I played alone outside, using a stick to draw pictures and patterns in the dirt. The grass had become very dry this fall.

Joshua had just left for his training.

The house was quiet and still. When Frank, our gardener, came by, he seemed to work without making any noise at all. His son, Paul, who usually plays and jokes, was quiet. As they raked the leaves and dry grass, the rakes said, shhhhh shhhhhh shhhh.

Vicky called, "Sarah! Sarah!" but even her call was soft.

I went in to dinner, just Mama, Dad, and me at the dinner table. No one felt like talking. Mama cut her food into many little bites but didn't eat them. No one had told me to wash up before supper, to tuck my shirt into my dungarees. They usually don't like it if I'm untidy.

"I built a kite today," I said. "Will someone take me to the beach to fly it?" Joshua would have done that with me.

Dad said, "Sure, honey. After we've eaten."

After dinner he examined the kite, tugging the string to test the strength of my knots. "It looks like a pretty nice kite."

"It's just old newspaper and sticks." Joshua had taught me how to make kites, but this was the first I'd made on my own.

"Let's test it out."

We were the only people on the beach. There was a

cold breeze. We sent up the kite; it caught the wind and stayed up. I ran and steered it.

"Look, Dad!" I shouted.

But he seemed to have forgotten all about me. He was staring out at the ocean.

Where Joshua would go. Way out across the ocean, to the war.

I stood still, forgetting the kite. It drifted to the ground.

"Get up."

The next morning: I stood over Lucca, who was still sleepy in his bed.

I was going to make things up to him. I was.

"Get up, little brother." I nudged him. He made a show of yawning and stretching. Then he noticed I was in my bathing suit and shorts. He hurried to get out of bed and get ready, too.

"We're not going to our part of the beach," I explained. "We're going to go to the big beach. Where all the other kids are. It's a day trip!"

Mom had not been especially pleased about my idea of a day trip without her. But I convinced her that it would be even *safer* for us to play where there were lifeguards and other families. And that compared to a few months ago, when she'd put me in charge of Lucca all the way to Florida, this was no big deal. "Keep your phone on," she said, finally giving permission.

I packed us a picnic, a beach blanket and towels, and sand toys. I covered us in sunscreen, and then we walked out to the trolley.

It still runs, the summer trolley I saw in Sarah's memory. The nearest stop was a couple of streets away.

I was a little worried that when I saw the trolley, I wouldn't be looking at something that was physically in front of me, but would instead be seeing a flicker of the past. What if I had us board a trolley from years ago? What would happen to us then? But Lucca, who, as far as I can tell, doesn't have my problem, gave a whoop and a holler when it was coming, and I let out my breath with relief to see it full of passengers with beach chairs and flip-flops and plastic beach buckets. Phew.

My fare was a dollar. Little guys like Lucca ride for free. We sat on a wooden seat slatted like a park bench. Lucca hung his hands out the open side when it started up, yelling, "Whooo whooo!" but I grabbed his arms to bring them back inside. The last thing I needed, after I'd convinced Mom this was a good idea, was for Lucca to tumble out. He hardly noticed, though, grinning as he closed his eyes against the warm breeze. I closed my eyes for a minute, too, trying to feel my brother's happiness. It was better than talking.

There were two boys my age sitting on the bench across from us. One of them smiled at me. I managed to smile back, but then the trolley stopped and I had to pick up our beach bag and help Lucca down from the seat, and by the time we got off the trolley I didn't see them anymore.

I set up our blanket near families with little kids. Sure enough, after a few minutes Lucca had joined a group splashing around in some shallow, warm pools that had collected when the tide went out. I didn't let him out of my sight, but I didn't hover. I just let him play. The other kids didn't seem to notice or care that he wasn't talking. He wasn't actually the only one, because some of the kids were younger and not really saying much, either. He fit right in. He splashed and got muddy in the smooth, gray sand.

Eventually I got up and paced around, an eye on Lucca, but also looking in the sand for anything left behind. I spotted an old chip bag, a crushed juice box, a plastic fork—but those weren't treasures. I collected them any-way, to throw out when we left.

I found a little bluish crab in a shallow pool and I called Lucca over to see. He loved the crab and tried to reach out to touch. "No, he pinches," I said. "See?" The crab pinched at the sand and brought his claw to his mouth, over and over. "He's having lunch."

Which reminded Lucca that *he* wanted lunch. He showed me by running to our blanket and dragging things out of the picnic bag. I had made us peanut-butter-and-grape-jelly sandwiches. Mom always tells me not to give Lucca peanut butter, in case he has an allergic reaction to it, but she fed me peanut butter all the time when I was little. Why all this care with Lucca and not with me?

Mom used to be more fun. We used to do things like take the train out of town to go hiking or explore other parts of the city. She used to take me to museums and let me wander around with a sketch pad while she worked. Now she was all worry-worry-worry and order-order-order.

Lucca seemed to love the peanut butter and didn't have any kind of allergic reaction. He smeared it all over his face. Luckily, I'd brought baby wipes, and I used a couple to clean him up. Then I rubbed more sunscreen on his face.

He ran off to play while I looked for more treasures. Nothing, though once everyone left for the day, the beach would probably be littered with little things.

But I'd promised Mom we'd be home by dinner. When a couple of families started packing up, I gathered our things and texted Mom to say we were coming back. As we headed up the boardwalk, we ran into an ice cream cart. "Let's spoil your dinner." Lucca jumped up and down, then picked a disgusting cartoon-character "ice cream" pop on a stick with bubble gum for eyes. He ended up with the neon food coloring running down his hand and his chin, but that was definitely okay by me. On the trolley home he was totally happy.

"You aren't still mad at me, are you?" I asked as I gently wiped him clean. "I'm sorry I was mean."

Lucca shook his head, rested it against my shoulder, and stayed like that for the rest of the ride.

• • •

I'd been reading, but my eyes kept closing, so I got up to turn off the lights. Then I couldn't fall asleep. I was drifting, listening to the gentle murmur of my parents' voices,

132

until they were no longer speaking gently; their voices had become sharp, sounding through the thin walls of the old house.

Dad said, "I'm the one who's burdening him? Anxiety? You're the one who's always worked up. Why can't you stop pushing, stop nagging? He'll talk when he wants to. He likes it here. He's happy."

"But doesn't it kill you, that you can't even get to know your own son?"

"Of course we know Lucca!"

"Then why isn't he comfortable talking to us? What *happened*?"

"I don't think anything *happened*! We've been talking about this for over a year. Just leave him be."

"You're giving up on him. You don't care."

"How can you say that?"

"Something's *wrong* with your little boy and you don't care."

"There's nothing wrong with him!"

I covered my ears.

Oh, God: Lucca.

I flew out of my bed and into his room. He was sitting up, the whites of his eyes shining big and round in the moonlight.

We reached for each other at the same time, and I hugged him. Then I set him down and turned around, throwing my hands behind me to be stirrups. He hopped onto my back, holding on loosely around my neck.

I left his room and went down the stairs, hoping we

wouldn't be heard. Luckily, the stairs felt as familiar to me as if I'd been running down them my whole life, so my feet never missed a step. At the bottom I opened the front door, carried Lucca off the front porch, and headed across the lawn. Then I set him on his feet and took his hand, and we ran down the steps and out to the beach.

Mom wouldn't have liked us going to the beach in the middle of the night. But who cared what Mom wanted?

Was it dangerous? The moon was bright, almost full, so we could see well. The tide was pulling back, leaving moist, freezing sand to chill our bare feet.

Lucca started shivering.

"It's okay," I said, knowing that the words wouldn't really make it okay. "Grown-ups fight. About all kinds of stuff. It's not your fault."

I sat down in the sand, pulling him into my lap and cuddling him.

"Why, though, buddy? Why don't you talk to us?"

I listened for his answer. I heard only the response of the waves, crashing and rolling loudly in the night.

"Is it Mom's fault?"

He shook his head.

"Dad's?"

He shook it again.

I couldn't bring myself to ask, *Mine?*

He must have been able to see the tears sliding down my cheeks, because he reached up to touch my face.

"Don't!" I turned away. "Your hands are sandy."

Then I pulled him into another hug, rocking him. "I'm sorry, I'm sorry."

After a few moments, I held him back at an arm's distance. "You *can* talk to us, you know. It would be okay."

Lucca looked at me, thinking hard. He clamped his lips, opened them, clamped them, opened them, took a deep breath, and said, "I just don't want to."

14

Men come in and out of the tent; some stay, some get treated. The medic comes back with a small dose of something and slips it into the girl's mouth. He gives me a blanket to wrap around her.

I sit with her. Holding her. Hold on, hold on.

Time passes. It might be days, weeks, years.

The little girl seems heavier and colder, and finally the medic says, *I'm sorry. I'm sorry, she's gone.* I don't respond. The child is lifted from my arms and taken away.

I don't move. Time passes. It might be days, weeks, years. Men come in and out of the tent; some stay, some get treated. The same medic comes back with an open can of something, something like stew, like always.

I hold on to the can and don't touch the food, don't touch it, just sit and sit and time passes and I hold the can and don't touch the food. It might be days, weeks, years.

Men come in and out of the tent; some stay, some get treated. I sit with the can and don't touch the food and don't touch it, and finally there's a hand on my forehead and the medic is there and he's saying, *Hey, soldier, hey there, soldier, I think you have a touch of fever, of fever, come on now, let's lie down, that's it now, a bed has opened, there's a good man.*

My head ached. I wanted to lie down so badly.

Where was I?

Sitting upright on our porch, leaning against the wall of the house, a beach towel wrapped around my shoulders. Lucca cuddled in my lap, sleeping soundly, his mouth open like when he was a baby.

Noise. The ache in my head became a pulse. What was Mom yelling about now?

She stormed out onto the porch.

"Siena!"

"What?"

"Do you have any idea what it's like to find your children missing in the morning?"

"Do you have any idea what it's like to be three years old and listen to your parents fight about you? Leave us alone."

She stormed off. But I knew she'd be very upset that Lucca had heard them.

There was no way I was going to fall back asleep now,

but I didn't want to risk waking Lucca, so I stayed right where I was, putting together the hazy memories of what had happened late in the night.

Had Lucca spoken to me? Had I imagined that? I had listened for, imagined him talking so many times.

Well, if it had happened, I definitely wouldn't be telling Mom and Dad. I wouldn't want them to believe that their fighting had made Lucca do it. If it had happened, he was talking to me and not to them.

After a few minutes, the door opened again. Dad sat down next to me.

"You guys heard that? I guess we figured you were both asleep."

"You were yelling loud enough to wake the dead."

"I'm sorry," he said, looking right into my face. "I mean it, he never should have heard that stuff. I'll tell him, too, when he wakes up." Dad rubbed his hands over the stubble growing in on his face. His eyes were red.

"I'm sorry, too."

"What are you apologizing for?"

I shrugged.

"I like it here, I do, and I do think it will be good for all of us," Dad said. "I just don't think that we should be focusing so hard on that one goal. It'll drive us all crazy when we could all be a lot more positive. And that would probably be the best thing for him anyway."

"Yeah, I get it," I said. "Sometimes Mom says just to wait, but then she tries and tries and tries."

Dad sighed. "I know. I think she's trying to convince herself it will be okay. Sometimes she feels calm enough to wait, but other times, she feels so much pressure, or guilt, maybe, that she isn't, that *we* aren't, doing enough. And then . . ."

He was quiet for a minute. Then, "It's because she loves you both so much, you know. She freaked out when she couldn't find you this morning, but I was thinking, They're together, and they're okay."

Dad rubbed at his face some more. He must have been really tired. "I have to get ready for work. Sure you don't want to be my assistant today?"

"Lucca," I said. "I want to be here for him today, you know, in case . . ."

"Right. Okay. I'm going to go get ready."

I held Lucca until he opened his eyes. He had a brief look of panicked confusion at being outside, but his eyes found mine and he relaxed.

"It's nice to wake up outside, isn't it?" I asked. It did feel good to be in the sunshine, surrounded by green leaves, though my back and neck were aching and I felt like I hadn't had a proper sleep in a month.

I took the beach towel off my shoulders, spread it on the wooden floor, and plopped Lucca down.

"Stay here, I'll get a surprise."

I went inside to the kitchen; in a few minutes I was back.

"Look, a breakfast picnic," I said, setting down two bowls of sweet but organic cereal.

Lucca dug in.

"Long nights make me hungry, too."

Dad came outside and held out his arms. Lucca went to him and was scooped up into a hug.

"I'm sorry, kiddo," Dad said.

I picked up the empty cereal bowls and went inside. I wouldn't ask Lucca whether he had really talked to me last night. What I'd thought he'd said was plenty of information.

• • •

Mom had calmed down. She snuggled with Lucca and then gave him a bath. I could hear them laughing together. She made us a nice lunch and the three of us sat down at the table to eat together.

After lunch I took a nap. When I got up, I still wanted to be by myself and not think about what happened last night. And there was something I could do—continue Sarah's story. I still needed to figure out what had happened to her. What could make a kid not want to talk?

I took out the pen and my notebook.

Jezzie was supposed to be here today. It was warm out, finally, so I wanted to play outside. But I hadn't seen her yet.

I sat on the porch with my dolls, waiting, waiting.

I kept my eyes up, looking over the railing, to see if she was coming.

Maybe if Joshua was home, he would have played with me. He used to make my dolls talk in very high, funny voices and say the silliest things. But Jezzie was all I had with him gone.

Frank was planting new flowers along the base of the porch.

"Got your eye out for someone?" he asked.

I nodded. "My cousin Jezzie."

"I saw Jezzie when I arrived."

"You did?"

"Yeah. That was a while ago. Not sure where she went off to. Maybe inside?"

"Maybe."

I took one of my dolls and went to look. Where would she be?

Nobody in the kitchen, but the sweet blueberry bread on the counter had been cut unevenly, with crumbs everywhere. I tasted them. Had Jezzie done this? Blueberry bread is Jezzie's favorite. Everyone knows that.

I walked through the first floor calling, "Jezzie! Jezzie?"

Would she go up to my room without me? She wasn't there, either.

What a puzzle.

I went out the kitchen door onto the back porch. No Jezzie.

I sat down and hugged my doll to my knees.

I started walking around the house and heard a small giggle and the rustle of clothes. The door to the basement was open a little.

Why would she be in the basement? That's where we mostly keep the things for the gardener.

I pushed the door open.

"Jezzie?"

And there she was, all right, with the gardener's son, Paul, their bodies close together, their lips pressed against each other's.

"Jezzie!"

She pulled back, surprised.

Paul turned pink.

This must have been Jezzie's idea. She always had crazy ideas.

"See you later," she told the boy, then grabbed my hand and started to run. I ran with her, holding tight to my doll in the other hand.

She led us all the way down the wooden steps to the beach, and when we got there, we both tumbled down onto the sand, out of breath.

"What were you doing?" I asked her again.

"Ah, nothing, Sarah." She propped herself on one elbow to look at me. "Just having a little fun. You won't tell anyone?"

"What if someone asks me?"

"Well, you could kiss him, too, if you wanted. Then I wouldn't tell anyone that you'd done it and we could both keep the secret."

"Nah, I don't want to."

Jezzie lay back with her hands behind her head. "You're a baby."

I lay back, too, looking up at the clouds. Jezzie was older than me, and she was probably right.

But not old enough that I would have thought she wanted to kiss Paul. Ew. Ew and yuck.

"Siena . . . Siena?"

I looked around and there was Sam, right in front of me.

"What are you doing?" he asked, his face scrunched up with worry.

"Writing." I tried to steady my breath. I felt woozy and put my head between my knees. It was not good to be interrupted while I was inside Sarah's mind, apparently. "I'm fine." I slowly sat back up.

"But I've been saying your name for like five minutes. It was like you couldn't hear me." Sam looked alarmed. "You just kept writing."

Great. Sam would think I was crazy, just like the kids at my old school. And he'd probably tell everyone about it. The same thing here all over again.

"I guess I just got really involved in the story."

Sam gave me a look. "It seemed like something more than that."

Sam pushed too much. I'd only known him a week, and yet he wanted to know things, to come over, to call. Maybe it was safer just not to have friends. They only turned on you.

"What are you doing here, anyway?"

"Today was my day to play with Lucca, remember? I just finished. Your mom said it was okay to find you."

I looked back at him. There *was* something about him that I trusted. He was nice about Lucca, and *to* Lucca.

"How was Lucca? He seemed okay?"

"Yeah, fine."

Sam stared at me, not about to let me off the hook. Okay.

"If I tell you, promise you won't think it's weird?"

Sam nodded. "Tell me."

I thought carefully about what version of the truth to give him, and how much. "I think my house is haunted."

"That's cool," he said very casually.

"You don't believe me."

"I'm as open to a good haunted house as the next guy. But what, are you being possessed to write?"

"No, it was my idea to start writing . . . but I don't control the story at all. It's like I'm just witnessing it, from the eyes of one of the characters. And it turns out the character lived here."

"Are you sure?"

"I think so."

Sam watched as I closed the notebook and set it beside me on the window seat. He was much more serious than usual. "Let's go."

"Where?"

"Outside?"

"Okay." Was he creeped out?

He watched me set the pen on the shelf.

"Hey," he said, seeing my collection, "this is that thing you found at the store." He picked up the butterfly hair clip.

"Yeah."

"You really aren't going to wear it."

I shook my head. "I won't ever wear it." I took it back and put it on the shelf.

"What's this other junk?"

"It's not junk . . . it's just stuff I found. Stuff that didn't belong to anyone anymore."

Sam didn't say anything else. He led the way downstairs.

"We're going for a walk!" I called to Mom.

"Dinner's at six!" she answered.

"Are you staying for dinner?" I asked Sam.

He hesitated; then, "Yeah, okay."

• • •

We sat down on the beach. Sam waited for me to talk. When I didn't, he asked, "Well, what is it?"

"What is what?"

"What you collect?"

"You just saw it upstairs."

Sam laughed. And laughed. I whacked his arm.

"Ow!"

145

"Why are you laughing at what I collect?"

"Oh." He stopped laughing. "It's totally random. Looking at it, you would never know, not in a million years, what it's a collection of."

"I told you, it's left-behind things. Things people didn't want anymore."

"That's a weird thing to collect." He paused. "Tell me again what happens? When you write, I mean."

I kept quiet for a minute, watching the sand dance across the beach in the wind. Finally I said, "I think it's all connected, the visions and what I collect. There's something left behind in the house . . . memories, feelings . . . and I don't want to leave them alone. Like I don't want to leave those little things I find alone." That wasn't answering him, exactly.

The wind picked up and whipped around us.

"I don't get it," Sam said. "What happens to you."

Well, I didn't get it, either.

We didn't talk for a few more minutes.

"So, how was playing with Lucca?" I asked finally.

"Good. We used his train set like last time."

"He seemed happy?"

"A little tired, but fine. Why are you so worried?"

"Mom and Dad had a big fight last night, about Lucca. About him not talking. He heard it."

"Oh," Sam said. "Does it bother you a lot, about Lucca?"

I sighed. "Kind of."

"Why?"

"Because . . . well, it's my fault Lucca's the way he is."

"Your fault?"

I made a small noise like a hiccup, and Sam scooted over and found my hand in the sand. He squeezed it. Our skin felt gritty and clammy; his hand was warm.

"He used to say things. Little things, like single words, two- or three-word sentences. He could name pictures of things in books or make the noise an animal makes. But he used to come to me all the time, to read books, to play, and it was annoying. He was noisy. I would be trying to do my homework or trying to talk to Dad. One day, when it was just the two of us, I yelled at him." Tears were sliding down my cheeks now. "To shut up and go away. I don't know how long it was after that, but he did shut up. And he didn't talk at all anymore."

Sam was shaking his head. "But brothers and sisters don't stop talking to each other forever because they yelled at each other once. My brothers and I would never talk to each other if that was the case. We tell each other to shut up all the time. Everybody does that."

"And I try . . ." I hiccupped again. "I try so much to show him I'm sorry, that I didn't mean it. I play with him and take care of him and read him stories every night."

"He knows, then. See, you have nothing to do with it. It's not your fault."

I brushed the tears off my cheeks with the back of my other hand so I wouldn't get sand in my eyes.

"Well, it's like a piece of my brother is lost, and maybe,

if I can't get it back but I take care of all these other things that are lost, Lucca's missing piece will come back to us on its own."

Sam and I sat, looking out at the water. Eventually he showed me his watch; we got up and walked back to the house.

Sam kept holding my hand. It was nice, not just the feel of his hand, but that when I told him about these things, he didn't run away. It was better than nice. Even if it seemed like he didn't one-hundred-percent believe me or think I was normal. He was still here.

He was still here.

Warmth flooded through me.

I suddenly thought of the difference between Sarah and Jezzie—Jezzie, who was grown up enough to be interested in kissing. Kissing. I gave Sam's hand a squeeze, imagined turning to him to kiss him.

But I couldn't do that, could I? Not if he belonged to Morgan.

15

It was raining. A perfect afternoon for reading and writing and thinking.

But Mom had other ideas.

"I have to do errands—boring ones, like picking out paint colors—and I thought Lucca would have more fun not going and he could stay with you."

"Great." I wouldn't mind spending time with Lucca—but Mom made it sound like a chore, one she didn't even ask me if I wanted to do.

So trancelike writing was out. It was so hard for people to get my attention once I started, Lucca probably wouldn't be able to.

"Get your rain boots," I told him. "Raincoat. Umbrella. We're going outside."

"Is that the best idea?" Mom really meant, *I don't think that's the best idea, but I'm going to pretend it's up to you to decide.*

"It's an excellent idea. It's not cold out. We'll go to Mrs. Lang's."

Mom decided she'd lost the battle.

"After the paint store, I'm going to the grocery store. I plan to have dinner on the table at six."

"We'll be back by five," I promised.

I didn't have cutesy plastic rain gear like Lucca—fireman's-red everything—but I put on my older sneakers and a Windbreaker with a hood. He made it back to the front hall in five minutes, looking excited.

"We're going to my friend's house," I explained as we walked down the beach along the water. Lucca seemed to like sinking his boots into the wet sand and listening to them squelch as he pulled them up. "She's old. Really nice. You'll like her and I think she'll like you."

By the time we got there, Lucca's boots were a muddy mess, and my sneakers would probably only be used for rainy days at the beach from now on. We stood with our feet on Mrs. Lang's doormat while we waited for her to answer the bell.

"Hello!" she said, very happy to see us. "You brought someone with you."

"This is my brother, Lucca."

"Hello, Lucca. Well, come in!" Then she laughed. "And *welcome* in!"

"Shoes off first," I said. Lucca took off his boots and I airlifted him into the house. Then I wriggled out of my own shoes. "We went on a muddy beach walk."

"Ah," said Mrs. Lang. "I used to like those. Now it makes the old bones too cold."

Lucca hung his coat on a chair and began to explore the house. He's okay at that. He doesn't touch anything, only looks.

"He's part of the long version," I said to Mrs. Lang, "of why we came here. The doctors thought it might help him for our family to move away from the city."

Mrs. Lang nodded. "Usually when something is wrong, people go to a city to see the doctors. Those must be very good doctors you went to."

"What do you mean?"

"They could have said he needed to come in every week, even if it wasn't true, just to get your money. If they want to send you away, it's a sign that they really care."

I hadn't looked at it like that before.

We watched Lucca zoom through the hallway and then disappear into another room.

"So what's the matter with him? He looks perfectly healthy to me."

"He doesn't talk."

"Oh, is that all?" Mrs. Lang laughed again. "No matter! All in good time! Let me see if I have any snacks that a little boy would like."

She found a bag of those vanilla cookies with vanilla cream—I like those so much more than Oreos—and fruit punch.

"I even have plastic kid cups," she said, collecting three

from a cabinet. "I bought them because I kept knocking my water glass off my nightstand and thought I should have something around that I couldn't break."

"That's smart." Then I noticed another cup, a small metal one, on the windowsill among seashells and little potted plants. It looked tarnished.

"Hey, where did you get this?" I picked it up. There were letters inscribed on its side, though they were hard to make out. It was oddly familiar.

"I found it on the beach years ago. Probably long before you were even born."

I held the cup for another minute.

"Are you all right?" Mrs. Lang asked.

"Yes. Can I have this?"

"What?"

"I think I know who it belongs to."

"You do?"

"It's hard to explain."

Mrs. Lang shrugged, which was not an answer.

Lucca returned to the kitchen.

"Want to play our game?" Mrs. Lang asked.

"I don't know that Lucca can handle Uno," I said. "But he loves Memory, if you have regular cards."

"I do," she said, "in the same drawer as the Uno cards."

I went to get them in the hallway. I could hear Mrs. Lang talking to Lucca about the cookies. Something she said made him laugh.

I came back with the cards and we all spread them out facedown on the table.

Lucca is extraordinarily good at Memory. We played for an hour and he won every game.

When we walked home in the rain, I could feel the little metal cup in my Windbreaker's pocket.

• • •

After dinner I found Mom washing pots in the kitchen.

"Where's the stuff you use to shine the old spoons?" I asked.

"Silver polish? Why?"

"I want to clean this up." I showed her the cup.

"Look in the big drawer."

I rummaged until I found it. Mom handed me a rag and gave me instructions, and I rubbed the polish into the cup until it shone.

As I did, the letters became clear. SEA. The ones on my pen.

My hands holding the cup went cold. It *was* the one Sarah had hidden on the beach for the treasure-hunt game the day of the dance, the one that her brother had never gone to find. But here it was, real, as real as the wallpaper.

I brought it upstairs and set it on the shelf with the other abandoned things. It seemed to belong there. It had come home after a very long time.

The open window made my curtains billow, as if I was being called to come sit in the window and learn more of Sarah's story.

Okay.

So I sat, held on to my pen, and let myself go.

Jezzie was back and Joshua was not.

It was a rainy, sticky sort of summer day. She announced that she wanted to work on sewing and make a little purse. I said okay, if she would help me thread the needles so I could sew, too. I got out our basket of fabric scraps and brought it to the parlor. She chose and laid out the pieces for her purse, designing a patchwork.

"That looks good, Jezzie."

"What will you make?" she asked.

"A dress for my doll." I picked out a couple of pieces to give it a patchwork look, too. I'm not good at sewing things, but if I made it a very plain-shaped dress—with no sleeves—it could be okay.

Mama came in while we were working and sat with us.

"Look what I'm making, Mama!" I held up my sewing.

She took it and made some adjustments. "Looks like a good start."

"What did you bring?" I asked.

She had a little basket, too. "Socks and stockings. I thought I'd do some mending. Make these things last longer."

She laid the items out in front of her in four piles—mine, hers, Daddy's, and Joshua's. She held a sock of Joshua's for a moment, then put it in the pile with the others that belonged to him.

"I think this one's yours, Jezzie," she said, holding up another sock.

Jezzie took it. "I can make a sock puppet out of it. Or a stuffed animal."

"If you want," Mama said. "Though I could teach you to mend it. It's a useful thing to learn."

"Nah, not right now," Jezzie said.

"You aren't so grown up, are you, Jezzie?" Mama smiled.

But Jezzie was grown up. Especially now that she was kissing boys. I opened my mouth to defend her. But Jezzie interrupted me, asking if Mama had buttons she could sew on the purse and use for eyes on her sock animal. Then she gave me a funny look, as if she'd guessed what I was going to say.

Mama told Jezzie to get the little button box. We sat and worked in silence. Eventually, Mama went to help Vicky with dinner.

"Hmm." Jezzie eyed Mama's purse on the table. She went over to look at it.

"What are you doing?" I asked as she pawed through Mama's things.

"Just looking at how the purse is made."

But she opened Mama's wallet and took out a ten-dollar bill. She didn't put it back in.

"Are you taking Mama's money?" That was an awful lot of money. Not like taking a dime to get candy.

"I have to have money in my purse, don't I? That's what a purse is for. She'll understand."

155

Something about it felt funny, but Jezzie made some sense. Mama had been helping her make her purse, and she would probably be willing to give Jezzie something to put in it. But a whole ten-dollar bill?

We continued our projects until we were called to dinner.

At dinner, everyone was quiet until Dad asked what we had been up to today.

Mama said, "The girls spent this afternoon sewing, working on projects they made up themselves."

"That sounds very nice," Dad said. "Maybe after dinner you can show me your projects."

"I was working on a dress for my doll. I'm going to make a heart to sew on right in the middle. And Jezzie was making a purse. At first she had nothing to put in it, but—"

Jezzie gave me a sharp kick under the table.

"Ouch!" I said. "What?"

This was the second time Jezzie had stopped me from talking. It was getting annoying.

"What's the matter, girls?"

"Nothing," Jezzie said. "She's just talking too much. I like things more quiet."

No one talked for the rest of the dinner. My parents are very cautious about Jezzie's ears. They don't want her to be in pain. They probably thought this was all about her ears.

But Jezzie's eyes were angry.

When I came back to myself, the whole house was dark and quiet. Everyone must have gone to bed.

I brushed my teeth, turned off my light, and lay down on my side.

Was I that different from Jezzie, taking things that didn't belong to me? I always told myself that they were left behind, unwanted. But some of those things someone might come back for. And Mrs. Lang hadn't actually told me that I could have that cup.

It took me a very long time to fall asleep.

16

In the morning, the cup was still there on the shelf.

I tried to ignore it and the guilt as I got dressed. Then I made my bed, something I never do, and sat down on it, facing the shelf.

Yes, it was still there.

"But doesn't it belong *here?*" I asked out loud. "It's not stealing if it belongs here."

Great. Now I was talking to myself.

This house was a loony bin.

And I still had so much more to learn. How was all this connected? What did it all mean?

It was the pen, and not the cup, that I picked up from the shelf.

"Come on."

Jezzie walked me through our yard and the next one

and then out toward the water—not in the direction you would go to swim at the beach. We stayed on the grass where the hill sloped out to dunes leading to the water without ever becoming a sandy beach. We ended up at the stone steps that went right down into the water. You could get in and out of boats there or just sit, resting your feet in the waves that made gentle lapping sounds against the stones. I didn't come here much, it being out of sight of the house. Jezzie probably had, and for that reason.

"Do you want Joshua to come back?" Jezzie asked.

I nodded. As she said his name a lump came into my throat. Things at home were awful without him.

"Well, you know, loose lips might sink ships. There are signs saying that all over town."

I nodded. I'd seen one of them outside the grocery.

"So that means," Jezzie continued, "if you want to make sure Joshua comes back, you need to stop talking. Haven't you noticed how quiet everyone has been since he left? A lot of soldiers don't come back. You don't want to take any chances that his ship will sink, do you?"

I shook my head.

"It's really hard not to talk—especially for little children like you—and we don't want you to forget. We need to lock your lips."

"Are you going to do it, too?"

"Of course not. He's your brother, not mine. It's you being quiet that matters."

"How do you lock your lips?"

"I have a key." Jezzie held up two fingers a couple of inches apart. "A special one."

"I can't see it."

"That's because it's invisible."

"How do you know it's the right invisible key?" I pictured her fishing it out of a whole box of invisible keys.

"Trust me. I know." Jezzie continued to hold the key in her fingers. "Just one turn on your lips and they'll be locked. And Joshua will come home. Ready?"

I didn't really want to give up talking. But if it meant that Joshua would come home, I'd do it. He'd asked me to keep a secret for him. He wanted me to keep quiet, too. I nodded.

Jezzie leaned toward me with the invisible key.

"Wait!" I shrieked.

"Are you ready or not? Don't you want to save Joshua?" I nodded again and stood still.

She pressed the invisible key to my lips and turned it.

Then Jezzie opened her hand as if she were tossing a pebble down the steps. Was it my imagination that heard something clatter on each stone step and drop into the water with a plop? That the water spread out in circular ripples?

Why had an invisible key done that? I opened my mouth to ask, but the words got stuck in my throat. I wasn't sure if Jezzie had noticed the strange thing that had happened.

Jezzie gave me a sweet smile. "There now, that's all

done with. Let's go have lunch. Do you hope there's jam or pudding today?"

But I couldn't answer her as we walked back up the dunes.

I came back to myself breathing hard. Whoa! What had Jezzie done? Could you, just like that, just like magic, take someone's voice away? That couldn't have really happened, could it?

I guess I had finally found out why Sarah didn't talk, but it hardly made any sense.

Well, what *did* make sense? How was it that I could even see this stuff? How did I know I wasn't making it up? Had I only made up this last scene because I was waiting for her to lose her voice? Had it really only come from my own imagination?

And what was with the invisible key? Why had it been invisible but audible, and how had it fallen into the water like that?

Arrgh! I had never had such confusing thoughts tumbling around in my head.

I stayed in the window seat, staring out at the water. Things looked almost exactly the same out there as they had in Sarah's time.

There was a knock on my door and it opened. Sam.

"Your mom says to come down for dinner."

"Already?"

"Yeah. You all right?"

"Yeah." I rubbed my eyes, which were tired and watery.

Sam lifted my notebook from the window seat and started flipping through the pages. "Can I read it?"

I took the notebook back and closed it. "None of it makes any sense, anyway."

We went downstairs and sat at the table. Four places set. "Where's Dad?" I asked.

"One of the kids had to go to the ER."

"Oh no, really?"

"Yeah. They aren't sure yet if it's a break or a sprain. They're taking X-rays. The parents met them there, but Dad feels like he should stay for a while."

We sat down to eat. Mom and Sam made polite conversation. I was as quiet as Lucca. I watched him scoop up noodles without a care in the world.

Maybe it really was my fault Lucca didn't like to talk. I was like Jezzie, taking things that weren't mine. Being mean to younger kids like I was to Lucca sometimes.

"Siena?" Mom asked. "Do you feel all right?"

I nodded, but she reached her hand over and felt my forehead. "You may be a little warm. Why don't you head right to bed after dinner?"

Sam caught my eye. I looked away, but I felt too bad to be embarrassed about my mommy checking me for fever and sending me to bed in front of him.

It was still light out, but I went upstairs, and without changing my clothes or brushing my teeth, I fell into bed.

17

The makeshift hospital with a couple dozen cots is full of people without names or faces. Where faces would be, their skin is smooth and blank. Their skulls and arms and legs are bandaged (or missing). No one is anyone. And because I am here, I, too, am no one. I, too, have no name, no face.

They send me a priest. I know because he wears a collar.

Hello, Father, I say.

Hello, son.

Can I ask you a question, Father?

Of course, my son, that's why I'm here.

What have they done to your face?

My face? He pauses, rubs his hand over his face. *Nothing has happened to my face that I know of. What do you mean?*

Your face, it's smooth and blank. No eyes, no lips, no

163

mouth. Just smooth and blank. How are you talking to me if you have no mouth?

He pauses for another moment before he says, *Try to be at peace, my son. Would you like to pray together?*

Yes.

But the prayers are blank, without words. The priest moves to trace his cross of blessing on my forehead, but I cannot feel his touch.

The doctor comes by and the priest moves to talk to him. I hear only the word *addled.* I think again, *How are they talking? Where does the sound come from if they have no mouths?*

Later the doctor says, *We've decided to send you home.*

Where's that? I ask.

The doctor checks my tags. *Maine.*

Is it nice there?

I've never been, the faceless doctor answers.

When I woke up, it was late morning. I could tell because of the sun's brightness and because there was no hustle and bustle in the house. Everybody must have left.

I sat up and looked at the clock. Just after eleven. Which meant I'd been asleep for . . . sixteen hours. And I'd had those dreams again, the war dreams. They made less and less sense each time. Nobody had had faces in this one.

Mom and Dad had just let me sleep through the whole

night and half the day. I didn't even know when Dad had gotten home.

I was hungry.

Mom had left a note on the kitchen counter. She'd checked and my forehead was cool, so she and Lucca had gone out to playgroup and the grocery store. *Back by two. Feel better!*

I crumpled up the note and threw it away.

Breakfast . . . breakfast . . .

Mom would probably say to have cereal and milk. Not interested.

I put together a breakfast sandwich and sat down to eat.

Was Sarah's story over now? Was that all I was supposed to know—how she'd lost her voice?

But why would that be something to know? Did people actually stop talking just because someone else didn't want them to? Was this house for kids who didn't talk?

The feeling around here hadn't changed at all. I had figured if I got to the bottom of the mystery, at least the house wouldn't feel like it had ghosts anymore.

I sighed.

I went upstairs, sat down in the window seat, and stared out the window for a moment, still thinking about how unchanged the view was.

There had to be more to this story. There had to be. I wasn't going to give up on Lucca, and I wasn't going to abandon Sarah now. What had happened to her next?

The weight of the pen in my hand—grounding, but

never too heavy—had become such a familiar feeling that it was somehow calming to me to pick it up and set to work.

Mama went through all kinds of feelings when I wouldn't talk.

First she thought it was a game.

Then she was angry. "Snap out of it, Sarah."

Then, after a week or so, she just seemed to be sad. She thought I was upset about Joshua being gone and decided to be understanding.

I started fourth grade. The teacher didn't like that I wasn't talking—my teacher from last year said that I had talked then. My new teacher had a meeting with Mama, and I don't know what Mama told her, but my teacher let me be.

Jezzie came by still, smirky and superior. She took my things and I couldn't say anything about it. Sometimes I wanted to punch her and shove her in the ocean.

Miserable as it was, the magic worked somehow. . . . We got a message that Joshua was coming home.

My heart was joyful to think my brother would be back. Nothing to worry about, then. So what if I could never talk again?

The day finally came.

Mama and Vicky had been cooking all day. The whole house smelled like pie. A happy smell.

My job was to tidy up Joshua's room. I dusted his desk, dresser, and windowsill; shook and aired his blue quilt outside; and put new sheets on the bed. I tugged and tugged the sheets and blankets to make sure everything was tight and smooth. There. What a nice room to come back to. A homey room because he was coming home.

Dad drove to pick up Joshua at the train station.

I waited by the front window. It was getting dark out. But there they were! The car's lights!

I wanted to scream out that they were here, but the sounds caught in my throat. Instead, I ran to the door and flung it open.

Joshua came up the steps first. I jumped up into his arms. His hug was stiff and he set me down again. He didn't even call me Little Bug. I looked up into his face, which seemed tired, yellowed, like he'd been sick. I looked into his eyes, but the laughing light that was usually there was dead. Dead.

Dad followed with Joshua's bag and set it down.

Mama and Joshua placed kisses on each other's cheeks, as stiffly as he'd greeted me.

Vicky came from the kitchen. "Welcome back!"

"We'll let you get washed up," Mama said. "And we'll have a lovely dinner together."

"If it's all right, I'll just have a sandwich," Joshua said. "I'll take it in my room."

At first, no one knew what to say. I felt angry. Didn't he know how we'd waited, how much we'd wanted him to come home? Didn't he want to be with us again? Didn't he know we'd had to save our ration stamps for the meat and sugar for his special dinner?

Then Vicky said, "You must be terribly tired from traveling. Of course I'll fix you a sandwich."

Joshua went directly upstairs.

Mama turned to me. "Have whatever you want for supper." And she went upstairs, too.

I was hungry. At least, I thought I was hungry. I followed Vicky into the kitchen.

I wandered around until I stopped in front of the pies. The pies that had taken all day to bake. Three of them.

"Here." Vicky handed me a spoon and left to bring the sandwich upstairs.

I went at the peach pie first, just eating big scoops straight from the middle. The filling was sticky sweet and goopy and almost too delicious. After I'd dug a huge hole in that pie, I went on to the next one, a berry one. I ate and ate, getting sticky red juice on my fingers and licking it off.

Then I started to feel not so good. I sat down on the floor, clutching my stomach. That was probably more pie than I'd ever eaten. I could have won the county pie-eating contest.

Dad came by, found a plate, and served himself portions of meat, green beans, potatoes. Then he spotted me on the floor.

"You have a stomachache? No wonder. You made fine work of those pies."

He sent me up to bed.

I curled up in a ball with my sick stomach.

But I didn't think I felt sick just from pies. It was the missing light from Joshua's eyes. Dead. Dead, dead, dead.

Joshua hadn't come home after all. Just an empty shell of Joshua.

From what I'd heard, Sarah hadn't spoken again, not even after Joshua had returned—was that because she'd felt like he hadn't?

So Sarah was missing her voice and Joshua his spirit.

And I was an expert collector of missing things.

But how was I to find these things? They were probably gone forever. And Sarah and Joshua would both be grown up by now—old, in fact, if they were still alive—and it was too late.

Not to mention that the things I'd collected had always been that—things—not spirits or voices. I'd never managed to get Lucca's voice back and I'd been trying and trying for ages.

I looked out the window, at the beach, at the water.

Now, how was it that we'd come to be here, in this place of many coincidences? That we came to a place with a history of not talking? What was it Mom had said? There were my dreams about the house, of course, but something had called to her here, too, even if she swore she couldn't sense the ghosts. She could, in her own way.

• • •

I needed to get out. I ended up pacing up and down the beach.

From far away, I could see someone walking. I should have recognized her from there, what with those curls blowing around in the wind, but when I got closer I was surprised to see that it was Morgan.

"Hi."

"Oh, hi."

"What are you doing out here?" she asked.

"I live just up there." I pointed to our house. "What about you?"

"I was just with— Oh, never mind."

She'd probably been with Sam. Why couldn't she just come right out with it?

"Hey." She took one of my hands and examined my nails. "I like this color. What is it?"

"Some kind of dark green. It's not black, either."

She laughed. "That purple one you had on before . . ." She paused. "Could I really borrow it?"

"You want to?"

"Yeah. It'd probably annoy Sam. Plus I like it."

"Ha. Yeah, okay." I led the way up the stairs to my

house, and then up to my room. "All my nail polish is out on my dresser."

Morgan paused at my collection. "What's all this?"

"Just . . . stuff."

"I see," she said, though she didn't. She started looking at the nail polish.

I handed her one of the bottles. "This is the one you liked."

"Thanks." She pocketed it. "I'll bring it back."

"Don't worry about it," I said. She went to head down the stairs. "Are you . . . ?"

"What?" she asked, turning back.

"Are you doing anything tomorrow?" I couldn't ask her what I really wanted to, for some reason, because I just couldn't get the words out, about her and Sam. So now I seemed like I wanted to make plans with her. Great. Maybe I was in for an entire day of bumping around questions I was too shy to ask.

"Oh." She thought. "Yeah, I'm busy. But maybe soon, okay?"

• • •

Eventually Mom and Lucca came home with the groceries. Lucca zoomed over to me, waving around some kind of craft project, two wildly painted paper plates stapled together and filled with dried beans, with colored streamers dangling from it.

"I think that needs a trip to the beach," I said.

Lucca jumped up and down and ran for the door.

Mom laughed. "I see you're feeling a bit better."

A queasy memory of not feeling well—and it having to do with Lucca—squirmed in my stomach. But I shrugged at Mom and hurried after my brother, who was already way ahead of me.

18

In the morning I had to watch Lucca so Mom could work.
I packed a big picnic lunch, dressed us both in bathing
suits, and got the big bag of sand toys.

We ran to the beach, where Lucca spun around and fell
down in the sand heaps, giggling and rolling.

I spread out a beach blanket and watched him run.

Suddenly someone plopped down next to me.

"Sam!"

"Your mom said you were here."

"It's true, we are."

"Are you better?"

"Yeah, I think so."

"What was the matter?"

I shrugged and smiled at him. Even if I could explain,
I wouldn't in front of Lucca.

When Lucca fell down, panting, and didn't spring back
up again, I said, "Let's build a sand castle."

It was probably the best sand castle I'd ever seen. Sam knew how to use just the right amount of water to pack the sand firm enough that he could stack bucket after bucket on top of one another. The towers ended up as tall as Lucca, who'd put himself in charge of building a wall around the castle, which he decorated with rocks. After Sam had constructed each tower, I smoothed it out, then traced designs and shaped turrets with my fingers.

When we were done, if Lucca had been talking, he would have said, "Wow!" I could tell by his bright eyes. He gave a whoop and jumped in the air and fell back into the sand, laughing.

"It's a great castle, buddy." Sam used his fingers to trace in the sand *Siena's Castle*.

We brushed the sand off our hands as best we could, and I unpacked sandwiches, corn chips, cantaloupe, and juice boxes. It was a great picnic, and I had packed enough food even though I hadn't known that Sam was coming.

"I like your sandwiches," he said. They were plain, just turkey and brown mustard.

"Thanks."

After we ate, we lay back on the blanket and watched the clouds. Sam and I said what we thought each cloud looked like, hoping that Lucca would tell us what he saw in the sky. But whatever he saw remained a mystery.

• • •

Sunday morning.

Extra sleepy, I slumped down to the kitchen.

Dad was there. It was nice when he was.

"Games?" I mumbled.

"What?" Dad asked.

"Do you have games?"

"Oh. Not today. Exciting, right?"

That made me start to wake up. Maybe we could do something cool together, like all get in the car and go somewhere. We could explore a different town or beach. I hadn't seen much of Maine at all.

But before I could even ask, Mom came through, all dressed and with a full laundry basket, on her way to the basement.

"It's Housework Day." Super-final, already-decided, the-last-word-on-everything.

"But it's the weekend."

"Only time we're all here to do it."

"But I've been sick."

"You seemed fine Friday *and* yesterday when you were out at the beach. Sorry, sugar."

I moaned and put my head on the table. Mom went on down to the basement.

"Hey, don't pout," Dad said. "You've at least got a good job."

"We have jobs?" Worse every minute.

"Yeah. I have to mow the lawn and make sure the basement is properly sealed so it won't flood if we get a lot of rain. And get some more paint-scraping done."

"What did I get stuck with?"

"You have to clean out the built-in china cabinet in the dining room."

"Clean it out? There's nothing in it."

"There's years and years of dust. Mom wants to put her nice dishes in it."

"That's it?"

"That's it. Not so horrible, is it? And things will look even better after you have some waffles with strawberries."

Probably true. Dad makes really good waffles with strawberries. The juicy, cut berries were already in a bowl on the counter. Dad poured batter onto the hot iron. In a minute, there was a pair of waffles for me, and in two minutes, a pair for him.

"Even Lucca has a job." He started eating.

"Really? What?"

"Sorting his toys. We've only been here a few weeks and his room's a disaster zone. Mom got him some colored bins to put everything in. Thomas toys in green, Playmobil in blue, blocks in red . . . He's throwing everything in, playing explosion, having a blast."

That was lucky. Getting a three-year-old to clean anything can be tough.

When I was done eating, Dad and I washed up. He gave me a special spray for the cabinet's wood and a different one for its windows and a whole bunch of rags.

I set to work. I have to admit, it was kind of fun. I shined up all the glass first and could see the improvement right away; Mom wouldn't be able to tell *me* to try my job again. The amount of dust that can settle inside cabinets is unbelievable. When I finally got around to wiping down the shelves, the rags quickly turned black.

I got up on a kitchen chair to clean the top shelf and reached one of the rags along the side, stretching all the way back. Something shuffled—thick paper. I slid it along until I could grab it properly.

It was a folded yellowed card. When I opened it, a black-and-white photo fell out. I picked it up and saw a girl with light hair pulled away from her face with some kind of ribbon headband. She wore a sweater with a button-up shirt under it. I flipped the photo over, but there was no name or date. She looked a little younger than me, maybe eleven.

I knew this girl.

I turned to the card. The front had typed lettering with neat script filling in the blanks. It was a report card written by Miss Jeremy, Grade Five, for the school year 1944–45, for Sarah Alberdine.

Sarah's report card.

I held my breath and opened the card, hardly believing what I was holding. Inside was a list of school subjects with names like Penmanship, Arithmetic, and Geography, with the letters S and E across from each. The letters stood for "Satisfactory" and "Excellent." There were more marked S than E. I flipped the card over to read the teacher's comments for November, March, and June.

November

Sarah is a good student who focuses well on her work. We are making every effort to encourage her to talk again, keeping in mind that her comfort in our school environment will be a primary factor. We understand that her difficulty is not a matter of intelligence, as demonstrated by her written performance.

March

Sarah continues to perform adequately in her written academics, but she seems unable to form close friendships with her classmates because of her unwillingness to communicate with them.

June

Sarah seems to have become more withdrawn as we approach the end of the year; we hope that the summer is restful for her and perhaps during the extra time with her family she will become interested in talking once again.

So it was all true. I had the proof. She'd continued not to talk.

There was nothing I could do. This had all happened already. It was all written. It was right here in my hands.

"Siena?"

"What?" I jumped a mile, then got a toppling feeling, a reminder that I was still standing on top of a chair, and grabbed the side of the cabinet.

"Are you all right?" Mom asked. "You look . . . greenish."

"Yeah. Yeah, I just think I'm still not feeling too good."

"Probably the cleaning supplies. Go get some fresh air. We can worry about the cabinets later."

I walked slowly up to the fresh air of my window seat, even though I knew it wasn't cleaning supplies making me sick. I gently set the report card on the shelf with the other abandoned things. Then I sat in the window, feeling the breeze play with the ends of my hair and my T-shirt.

What would be the point of going into Sarah's story again? There was nothing I could do for her. That had all been so long ago.

I had to watch these things unfold, but there was nothing I could do.

Nothing.

• • •

The rest of the day was quiet. I didn't hear from Sam at all, and I'd gotten used to hearing from him or seeing him almost every day. Was he with Morgan? He must have been.

The gloominess of not being able to do anything for Sarah, or for my brother, clung to me like heavy, invisible clothes.

I even started to feel a little sniffly.

"Maybe you are still sick," Mom said to me at dinner.

"Just a summer cold. Let's get her some extra vitamins," Dad suggested.

Lucca said, "Puh . . . puh—puh—puh."

We all looked at him. Could that be "puh, puh—pass the ketchup?" or "puh, puh—please?" or "puh, puh—potatoes?"

Then he zoomed his fork around his plate. "Puh, puh, puh."

We got unexcited again.

• • •

I was lying on my bed staring at the wall when Mom came up to the bathroom and started unpacking a drugstore bag. "It's nice to see your door open for a change."

Hmm. I hadn't realized I'd left my door open. Or even that I usually didn't. It was true, though.

"I got things for you. Come see."

What embarrassing things had she bought me from the drugstore?

"Here." She placed three tubes of lip gloss in my hand.

"Why did you get so many?"

"Because I didn't know what you'd like." She sounded sad, as if she thought she should have known what I would like. But how could she, when I didn't know either? She watched me staring at the colors and, with a look of affectionate exasperation, picked one of the tubes back up to unwrap the plastic. "Try them." She started unloading lotion and sunscreen from the bag into the medicine cabinet.

I tested each color on the back of my hand. "I like this one."

"You do?" Mom looked at me with an expression so soft and pleased it made my heart ache. I regretted telling her I liked anything. I didn't wear makeup. She did. I didn't want her to think we were close now just because she'd gotten me some makeup.

"Sit down," she said.

I shut the toilet lid and sat. She took the gloss from me and applied it to my lips.

"I think it's nice." She handed me a small mirror from the counter. It was nice. But still . . .

"Is this about Sam?"

Mom waited a moment before answering. She looked almost hurt. "No, sweetheart. It's about you. I just thought you'd like some lip gloss."

I rolled the tubes in my palm.

Mom knelt in front of the toilet and pulled me into a hug. She felt like my mom, the one who used to do fun things with me. I didn't hug her back, but just for a moment, I rested my head on her shoulder.

• • •

I was in my room thinking and missed Lucca's bedtime again. I was doing that a lot lately. When I tiptoed to brush my teeth, I overheard Mom and Dad whispering through the open crack of their bedroom door. Lucca wouldn't be woken by it and I had to hold my breath to hear properly.

"In the reasonable part of my brain, I know that nothing needs to be different and things might still turn out okay, but I can't help feeling . . . disheartened." Mom was sadder than she ever sounds when she talks to me about Lucca.

With Dad always at camp and games and Mom scrounging to find time for her work and trying to fix up the house, things didn't actually seem less difficult than in Brooklyn.

Mom continued, "If he's not going to talk . . . I wish I could go inside him, to hear his thoughts . . . to help."

"He'll talk when he's ready," Dad said gently.

I tiptoed on, extra quiet so they wouldn't realize I'd been standing there. I shut the door to the bathroom and brushed my teeth, wondering about what Mom had said. If she got in Lucca's head, she might see all his memories and she would know what I had done to him.

I moved the toothbrush in very slow circles, feeling like there was too much saliva rushing into my mouth. Like that feeling you get before you get sick. I quickly spit and rinsed.

Mom couldn't really see Lucca's thoughts. Or anyone's. Normal people can't do that. Only wackadoodles like me.

I went back to my room and turned off the lights but sat up in bed with the sheet drawn over my knees. I didn't feel like sleeping.

I had hoped that by figuring out what had happened here, I'd also be helping Lucca. Now the report card . . . it confirmed that Sarah's life was set in stone.

A dead end.

But . . .

When I visited Sarah's life, it was as if it was still present, still going on, on some level. Did that mean that there *was* something I could do?

Could I go inside her and also safely be myself? Not just watch, but act? I had never been able to do that before; I was always frozen, just observing, while my body clung to my pen and wrote. Could I go one step further?

And if I went within her, to use her body to be myself, I wouldn't be able to talk to Sarah herself. I would have to talk *through* her, to someone else.

To Jezzie? But I didn't know what to do but threaten or scare her, and I wouldn't be sticking around to follow through, so it would be meaningless.

Who else would it make sense to talk to?

Not a grown-up, obviously.

Joshua.

Maybe I could reach Joshua. I knew things about what he had gone through that no one else in the world knew. I had seen them through his eyes. I had been there.

But what if, in slipping into Sarah as more than just an

observer, I broke something? What if I got stuck there, if I couldn't come back?

I lay down, a feeling of resolve washing over me, and with it, exhaustion.

Could I really do it?

Tomorrow night I would try to see if I could put myself into Sarah. But for tonight, I would sleep.

19

I spent the next day nervously pacing, but Mom decided not to say anything this time. I walked circles in my room; I walked up and down the stairs; I walked to the window in Lucca's room and looked out; I went outside and traipsed around the house.

Another day without Sam. Was it Morgan? Had she told him to stop spending so much time with me? But I wouldn't have been good company anyway. I was so focused on trying to think up how to visit Sarah and get all the way through this time.

When evening finally came, I lay down in my bed. I left the light on, closed my eyes, and thought of being in Sarah's body, a different body. Then I stopped thinking.

That was when the lighting in my room changed, become softer.

I opened my eyes.

The wall color had changed, too; it was almost the color of my nightgown.

I gasped and sat up. Wait. I wasn't wearing a nightgown! Yes, here were my pink polka-dot shorts, my old T-shirt. The yellow striped wallpaper. I dropped back on the bed, sweating. But then I calmed down and felt a little excited: I had done it. For a moment, I had gone into Sarah without the pen, just on my own.

My brief excitement faded; I hadn't really liked the feeling of being in someone else's body.

What happened to me, the me-me, when I was inside somebody else?

•   •   •

Over the next few nights, I got through enough so that I could see the old-fashioned, Sarah's-time version of my room and give the fingers of Sarah's body a good wiggle, but then I would hear Sarah's voice cutting through, flowing with a dreamlike quality that told me I had entered while she was sleeping. I would be there, too, still me, still thinking, but my hand knew it wasn't connected to anything back in my own world, and I would feel for the bed beneath me in a panic, for the pajamas I was wearing, and fully come to in my own body, in my own time, my heart racing and my breathing fast.

And the longer I spent there, the harder and harder it was to come back. When my mind went to look for my own body, it drifted, so familiar were the sensations of being within myself that I didn't know how to call them up.

Even so, after a few days, I decided that it was time. There was no more sense in practicing. I would have to take the plunge, go all the way in, and climb out of that bed in another time.

Tomorrow.

• • •

Sam had been playing with Lucca and asked me to go for a walk on the beach after.

"Sure," I said, though I was thinking less and less of things here, in my own time.

"You're all quiet," Sam pointed out as we walked along.

"Just thinking."

"About what?"

I didn't answer but watched the waves crest and fall, crest and fall.

"Siena?"

"I feel like I might not come back," I whispered.

"What are you talking about?"

Was what had happened with Kelsey going to happen again with Sam? Would he learn too much about me and want to run away?

But he made me want to tell him things. He made me feel safe.

I shook my head. "I just . . . have to go away a little, and I don't know how easy it will be to get back."

"What do you mean, a little? Like a trip?"

I shook my head again. "The ghosts—"

"Siena, what are you talking about?" Sam hissed, seeming like he wanted to shout but unable to put the strength in his voice. He looked stricken.

"The ghosts—"

"Stop saying that!" Sam yelled, then lowered his voice. "You aren't going to hurt yourself?"

"No, nothing like that." I sighed, wishing I hadn't brought it up at all. Maybe this *would* be like Kelsey all over again. "Never mind."

• • •

I read Lucca his bedtime stories, *Goodnight Moon* and *Frederick*. He cuddled against me, and I enjoyed his warmth.

Was I giving him up, to try what I was going to do? Could I get stuck if I was there too long? Would this be the last time I saw my own brother?

But this had to help him, right? Even if I didn't get back to see it? If I tried so hard to help Sarah and Joshua, wouldn't that somehow fix things for my brother, too?

I kissed him good night, tucked him in, and went back to my room and sat in the windowsill, waiting for Mom and Dad to come up to bed, listening for the house to be quiet. The sky deepened as I sat; the stars came out and brightened.

My body—that wasn't exactly me, right? The me-me was deep inside. That was the part of me that would go on the journey tonight. What would happen to my body while I was gone? What would hold me to it?

Finally all the lights were out; the house grew quiet. It seemed like everyone was in bed.

I climbed into my bed, too, and lay flat. I tried to breathe deeply, to relax my mind. I let my worries go, one by one. I tried to keep my mind present and let go of my body. I could do this. I was Siena, certain, and strong, and brave. I *was*.

I blinked. I must have been dreaming, and this must be waking up.

There was no use lying awake at night, in the loneliest hours of worry. Sometimes I could hear Joshua crying, or Mama crying. That was probably how I would end up, too, waking at night: crying.

I held on tight to the sleepies, and drifted. Something was calling me back there, asking me to stay asleep.

She was right. I came to enough to know. I was saying over and over—*praying* over and over—*Stay asleep, Sarah. Stay asleep.* What I had to do was an odd mix of letting myself go and grasping onto myself just a little.

Please stay asleep, Sarah. I need to borrow your body, but I'm trying to help you. I will give it back to you. This will help you, and Joshua, too.

And the part of Sarah that usually took over as soon as I slipped in to share her memories, the one that directed all her thoughts and movements, seemed to stay asleep. I would make the decisions this time. I was ready.

I started first by relaxing, just flexing my fingers, one at a time, like I'd tried to practice in those brief sessions earlier this week. It's really hard to flex your toes one at a time, but I gave them a good wiggle. Next step: I climbed out of bed, standing on steady feet, but feeling shorter than in my own body. It felt odd controlling Sarah's body so actively—it was familiar, from being in her memories, but it was definitely different from mine; her arms and legs didn't reach as far as I was used to. Was the stomachache hers or mine? We seemed to share the same whirring feeling of anxiety.

Our room was familiar, even though I think it took more footsteps to get across the floor. The doorknob seemed higher from Sarah's perspective. The doorknob itself was different . . . an octagon of glass instead of round metal.

I remembered which room was Joshua's: the empty "guest room" in my time. I tiptoed across the hall and opened the door, slipped inside, and shut it behind me.

He was sleeping fitfully, muttering.

"Joshua," I said, but my voice, or Sarah's voice, I guess, was gruff from not talking for a long time. I cleared my throat. "Joshua."

He still didn't seem to hear. I walked over and stood right at the end of the bed. I gave a hoarse, sharp whisper: "Joshua!"

He jumped, sitting straight up in bed, gasping, frantically looking around. Then he realized he was in his own bedroom, recognized the outline of his little sister in the dark. His breathing slowed and he lowered himself back down to his pillows. "Go away!"

"Shhh. Someone will hear you."

"Go away, go away!" He cried now, into his pillow. Then, in a weak whisper, "Go away, please, go away!"

I didn't think he was talking to his little sister anymore. To his memories? To things that were not here in this room with us, but far across the ocean?

"I know . . . I know about William, the little girl and her family, the people without faces . . ."

"What are you talking about?"

"I saw it, too."

"How could you have?"

"I dreamed it."

He opened his eyes. They widened in surprise. "I can see your face! Clear as anything! My Little Bug . . . but you don't talk like her."

"I . . . I'm not really Sarah. Not inside."

"Who are you, then?" Joshua sat up.

"I'm Siena."

My name lingered in the air for a moment. It did sound strong, and beautiful.

"Siena? What kind of name is that?"

"Mine."

He closed his eyes; his brows scrunched. "It's familiar, somehow."

We both thought for a minute.

"Where did you fight in the war?" I asked.

"Italy."

"You might have seen my name before, then. On a map. Or maybe you have even been there."

"Is that where you come from?"

"No. I actually come from right here, like you."

"What do you mean?"

"I can't explain it. I live years from now in this house, but I can see the past. I saw what you went through. You found the little girl in the ruined house and you carried her . . . carried her all the way to a doctor, but she died."

"Stop it. You can't know that."

"But I do. You're hearing me say it."

"Who knows what I'm hearing? I can't trust what I see and hear anymore."

"The whole world changed on you. Probably there's nowhere that feels safe."

I slid over closer to the bed and took his hand. He flinched at first. With our hands touching, I could feel us connecting inside, too. At first I felt scared, but I willed myself to relax so Joshua could, too. Something flowed between us.

"It *is* like that," he said. "Even when the memories aren't active in my mind, there's that fear. It's always creeping, round and round my heart."

"I feel that way a lot, too."

"Have terrible things happened to you?"

I thought about that. "No. I guess I just feel like I don't know what's real, because unexpected things happen to me, and where and when I'm from, you feel like something awful could happen at any time and you wouldn't be ready."

"But I got ready. And it didn't help."

I rubbed the back of his hand with my thumb, trying to keep him calm, to try to make him see that I understood.

Maybe he was sick—but I felt the core of my being, in pulse with Sarah's beating heart in the chest I visited, think of him gently, the way a sister treats her brother when he needs help. *That* was the connection I felt. Like when I had sat with Lucca earlier.

"Why are you here?" When I didn't answer, he asked, "What do you want?"

"To help you and Sarah."

"Why? Why do you care?"

"I just . . . do. I want you to be okay."

"But why?"

"I guess it has something to do with me and Lucca."

"Who's Lucca?"

"My brother."

"His name is familiar, too."

"He doesn't talk, my brother. It's like there's something in the way between us. I try and try but I can't fix it. You and Sarah have the same thing."

"What do you mean?"

"Haven't you even noticed? Sarah doesn't talk anymore!"

"What do you mean she doesn't?"

"Jezzie took her voice."

"What did she do with it?"

"She threw it in the ocean."

For the first time, Joshua laughed.

"What?" I didn't see it as something to laugh at.

"How is that even possible? I always knew there was something wrong with that Jezzie. She must be a nutty spirit like you on the inside."

I felt a little flame of anger. "Hey! I'm here to help you!"

"So you say."

"It was for you, you know. Sarah gave up her voice for you so you would come back safe." It was like he didn't even care. I wanted to throw his hand away from me in disgust, but I still felt that charged energy, that love, that flowed from both Sarah and me. If I took that away in anger, I'd be giving up on him.

"I can hardly follow you."

"Jezzie told Sarah you would only come back if she stopped talking, and she believed it. Now you're here and you won't even look at her. How's that fair?"

"I still don't see why you care. Why it's your business."

I started to tell him more about Lucca, about what I said to him that one time long ago before all the problems started, but also about how much fun we have, playing at the beach, getting him ready for bed, just being together, even without him talking. I talked about it for such a long time it seemed that the stars had shifted in the sky I could see through the window.

When Joshua spoke again, his voice was softer. "Sarah and I used to be close like that, too. When I picked up that little girl, I was thinking of Sarah, hoping she was all right."

"So help her. If you come back to your family, you don't have to lose each other, too. Do you know what's going to become of them without you? Sarah's never going to talk again, and your parents are going to fall apart. So please, please, get up. If you stay here like this, you'll only relive the same bad memories over and over, instead of making good new ones. What about your family? Don't you want to see their faces again?"

His breathing and hand relaxed a little more. He was getting close to sleep again.

"What for?"

"You just have to keep going. To keep them going, too."

"I . . . I could try."

"You *could*. . . ."

"Maybe. If I don't?"

"I might have to come here again."

A smile stretched across his face. "I think I would like that."

"I don't know if I *can*," I said seriously. "Not like this. It might be putting me and Sarah in danger. But what will happen if you don't is what I told you: all the people you love are going to fall apart. Their lives will be full of the darkness you've brought home. They will remain faceless to you. But if you get up, if you try to let a little of it go, if

195

you make new happy memories, you can have them back. If you remember me, you can remember this again any time you want, in your mind. Or maybe you could visit me in my life."

"You think so?"

"I do." And I did. After all, I'd been visiting Sarah. "Just listen for me, my spirit in this house. Sit near the window. Be ready to write things down. You should be able to find me."

"Really?"

"Really. You just need to believe it's possible."

"You are pretty crazy. Or I'm crazy for thinking you're here."

"If it gets you out of bed, it's okay by me."

"Okay."

"I don't know how long I can stay." I gave his hand one more squeeze. "I think you have everything you need."

"Where *is* Sarah? If you're in her body, where is she?"

"I don't know." A feeling of panic for both Sarah and myself coursed through me.

"Get going, then. Switch back."

I nodded. "You'll get up?"

He nodded back.

I let go of his hand.

"The next time you see Sarah and she *is* Sarah, tell her that the spell is broken. Jezzie's spell. She might even be listening, know already. Tell her she can talk now. You can get her to talk again."

Joshua nodded.

"What about Lucca?" he asked.

"I'm not sure. I've tried so many things."

"What did you say Jezzie did to Sarah? Do the opposite thing, and maybe Lucca will open up. You never know."

Then he seemed to drift back to sleep. Maybe he'd think the whole thing had been a dream.

Can two people in different times meet in their dreams? No reason why not. No reason.

20

Now the hard part: getting back.

Could Sarah have gone to my body? Traded places? I'd had to think hard to get here, so I guessed she could only go there if it was on purpose.

I walked back to my room—in Sarah's time, so Sarah's room—well, our room. I lay down and buried my head in the pillow, but it didn't smell like my pillow, though the smell was familiar. I tossed and turned. I wasn't leaving.

Sarah, come back. I'm ready to go.

But I continued to lie there.

It was a sleepy summer day, the kind when you don't even want to move. I went out to the porch and lay back on the swing, my tiptoes touching the floor enough to make the swing sway back and forth.

Jezzie came by. I shut my eyes as if I were really asleep.

"Sarah," she said. "Sarah!"

I kept my eyes scrunched closed and pressed them extra tight when she shook the swing. I let my arms and legs go loose like jam.

"Huff!" She must have been convinced I was sleeping, because she left. I peeked my eyes open to check and saw her leaving the yard. I tipped my head back to stare up at the ceiling but found there was someone standing over me.

My brother. He was looking down at me, into my eyes.

"Hey, Little Bug? Is there room for me?"

Of course there was! I sat up and stretched my arms to him as he sat down. I pressed my face into his shirt and felt it grow wet with tears.

"Good work pretending for Jezzie. You aren't such a little bug anymore, are you? How have you been?"

I shook my head and cried harder.

"You can tell me. I'm here now. Please?"

"Siena, honey? Siena, wake up."

Mom.

I drifted from Sarah. I wiggled my fingers, trying to feel if they were mine. Mine-mine. I dared to peek open my eyes.

"Mom!" I sat up and hugged her.

"Hey there," she said, patting my back. "Hey. Are you okay?"

"Yeah."

"I was worried. I couldn't seem to wake you up."

"Yeah, I was . . . Well, anyway, I'm back now."

"Back?"

"Never mind." I was so relieved, I was shaking. My mother had brought me back. Here we both were, sitting in my bed. "What—what are you doing in my room?"

"Sam called. Which was weird, it's so late . . . almost midnight . . . but then he sounded scared or something. He asked if you were here, and I said you'd talk to him tomorrow. Then he said, 'Could you just go check on her?' I peeked in here, and you seemed to be sleeping, but something in his voice . . . He mentioned ghosts. Are you still on about that?"

I listened, I felt the air. It was still. Normal.

"No. I'm not worried about them anymore."

"That's a relief. Is that all he was worried about?"

"I guess."

Mom kissed me on the forehead. "I'm glad everything's okay. I'll call him back."

I felt exhausted, ready to fall onto my pillows for a good sleep. "And I know now."

"Know what?"

"How people, you know, keep going even when something terrifying might happen at any time."

"How's that?"

"You have strength inside you. You can do anything."

Mom laughed gently. "I think you're still asleep. You don't talk like that when you're awake."

And I might have been; I could barely make her out anymore, even though she was sitting right in front of me.

"Go, honey. Go to sleep."

And I went.

21

When I came downstairs in the morning, Mom was reading something at the kitchen island.

"Check the porch," she said without looking up.

"Huh?"

"The porch. Sam's here."

I headed outside.

"Hi," I said, suddenly very aware of my pajamas. I sat down next to Sam. He had an empty bowl and spoon. "I see you've been cereal-and-milked."

"Everything . . . okay?" Sam asked.

"Yes."

"You sure?"

"Yes."

"One hundred percent?"

"Yes! Except that I'm wearing my pajamas." I got up, but then I turned around and gave Sam a hug, even though he was still sitting down.

"What?" he asked.

"You're checking on me."

"Yeah, so what?"

"So what nothing." I smiled. "Thanks for calling last night."

He didn't return my smile.

"What?" I asked.

"You scared me. It's . . . creepy."

"Hey, look, I'm sorry I scared you. I'm all right. I think everything's okay now. I'm going to get dressed. Don't leave."

I jumped into some clothes and grabbed my sneakers.

"Let's get real breakfast," he suggested when I returned. "I have money."

We walked to the center of town, to the diner. I ordered an omelet with green peppers and onions, and rye toast and grapefruit juice.

"Hungry?" Sam asked.

"Starving."

He shouldn't have talked, what with his bagel and bacon and cheddar-cheese eggs.

When the food came, we got right to work eating.

"Tell me what happened with the ghosts."

I told him, as best I could, about what had happened. He listened, raising his eyebrows at points.

"You must have dreamed that whole thing," he said.

"I don't care whether it was real or not. I think it helped."

"And you think this will help Lucca?"

I nodded.

"I o no," Sam said, his mouth full of food.

"What?"

He swallowed. "I don't know. Why would it have anything to do with Lucca?"

"I helped them. Something should help me."

Sam was quiet. I assumed he was thinking about our conversation. Then he said, "I should order some orange juice."

"Sam!"

"What?"

"What do you think?"

"Oh, about Lucca? You're talking, like, about karma or something, right? What goes around comes around? You did something good, so you'll get good back?"

"I guess so."

"What if the good is something else? Why would it have to be related to Lucca?"

"Because the ghost puzzle and the Lucca puzzle *are* related. They're connected, I know it. We came here for a reason." What was it Mom had said? She had a feeling something here, something on the beach, would help Lucca? And why, why had I dreamed about the house long before we were even thinking about moving?

I knew that Mom's feelings were just regular feelings, not psychic ones. But they still meant something. Something had reached out and pulled us here from a long way away. Something that she could only vaguely sense, and something that only I would perceive.

We finished up our food.

"Want to hang out?" I asked Sam as we left the diner.

"I can't. I have to go home. Mom wants to have a 'family day.' Usually that means we play a board game and watch a movie."

"That's okay. Thanks for the great breakfast. And thanks for coming by this morning."

As I walked back I couldn't get what Mom had said out of my head, about something at the beach helping Lucca. Why?

It must have been connected to last night. . . .

Joshua had said maybe I could help Lucca by doing the opposite of what Jezzie had done to Sarah. But how would you do the reverse? What had happened hardly made any sense.

I stopped walking, closed my eyes, and pictured that moment in Sarah's life, Jezzie turning the invisible key and tossing it down the stone steps. I remembered the taps the metal made on the stone, heard the splash it made when it hit the water, saw the rings ripple out from the spot where it fell.

I started to have an idea, a crazy, impossible idea.

It was worth a try, anyway. Wasn't everything already crazy?

When I got back to our house, I headed out down the path I had never been down before, not in this time, anyway. I tried to follow the way Jezzie had led Sarah, across the grass and over the dunes. The ocean grew closer.

There! There were the steps leading into the water. They were real. Just like everything else had turned out to be.

I took off my shoes and sat on the lowest dry step with my feet in the water. So cold!

What would I find? What I was looking for was invisible.

I scanned the water with my eyes, not wanting to stir up any of the sand and make it cloudy. I studied the sand and the long reeds of dune grass. They were very hard to see through.

The grass scratched my toes as I started to walk through the shallow water, carefully lowering my feet to each step. Each was more slippery than the one before it. When my feet hit the sandy bottom just off the last step, I was standing about thigh-deep in the water.

I couldn't see anything. But, again, I was looking for something invisible . . . I closed my eyes. I *listened*.

To the sound of water lapping against the stone.

To the wind rippling so very quietly through the grass along the dunes.

To the air itself.

I listened for things that no one would expect to hear. *I* could hear them.

Things I could feel, but not yet see . . .

I trailed my icy toes through the sand, searching, searching. After a few minutes, I felt something. Not rock or plant. It was metal. Small. I held my breath. Keeping my eyes closed, I reached down and felt through the sand until my fingers found it, too. I gathered up the object and brought it to the surface.

Only then did I open my eyes. Through Sarah's eyes, I hadn't been able to see it. With my own, I could.

In my hand was a little key. Bronze-colored with black patches, a Celtic-knot handle, and two skeleton teeth at the tip. Shorter than my pinky.

Maybe this was it.

Maybe this key would help my brother.

22

That night, I waited until I was sure Mom and Dad were asleep, and then I slipped into Lucca's room and quietly closed the door behind me.

Lucca's a deep sleeper; he used to fall asleep in his stroller on the street in New York, ignoring sirens and car horns, subway trains and street music. When I sat down next to him on the bed, he slept on.

He had that sticky look of little kids who sweat in their sleep. His Batman pajamas clung damply to his skin and his bangs were moist; his mouth hung open, his chest gently rose and fell. I smoothed his wet hair away from his face.

"Hey there, dreamer," I whispered, "with all your thoughts so secret."

I turned the key over in my hand. The bronze gleamed in the moonlight. The key was so solid, so real to me. Jezzie had made Sarah *believe* she could take her voice away, and that had been the important thing. If Jezzie had been able to use the key to convince Sarah it was wrong to talk, maybe I could use it to let Lucca know I wanted him to. And maybe soon, he'd want to.

"Hey, little brother," I whispered.

I shook his shoulder gently, and he opened his eyes. As he woke he examined my face in the dark.

"I just wanted to tell you . . . I'm sorry . . . about how I made you feel . . . about talking, I mean. If that's not why you haven't been talking to us, I don't want to change you, not if you don't want to. But I would love for you to talk to me, and Mom and Dad; to go to school and play with the other kids. Maybe that doesn't seem like so much fun to you, but it can be. So anyway, think about it."

I rolled the key in my fingers. Lucca sat up.

"Just if you want to," I promised. "I brought something to help . . . a magic key."

I held my hand out to show him. His night-light gave enough light to see it, but he held his own hands up, empty, and shook his head.

He couldn't see the key. It seemed only I could. I'd dreamed it, believed it hard enough that it had become real just for me.

"That's right," I said. "It's magic. It's invisible."

Lucca stared at me.

"Okay?" I asked.

He nodded.

I pressed the key to his lips and gave it just a hint of a turn.

I sat looking at him for a little bit longer. Maybe this would change everything. But it would only matter if it was what Lucca really wanted.

He cuddled back down onto his pillow. I stayed until he was asleep again. Then I went back to my own room and set the key on my shelf with the other abandoned things. That was the end of what I could do—it would be up to Lucca now, to choose his own way.

23

I finished getting dressed in the morning and headed down to the kitchen, where Mom had put out a box of fruit-rings cereal. I poured myself a bowl.

Lucca came downstairs. He still had that sticky, sleepy look.

"Hey, buddy. How are you?"

He climbed up into the chair next to me. I crunched my cereal for a minute and then realized he'd probably want some.

I dumped a dry handful out on the table. "Wanna play colors? Can you eat a pink one?"

Lucca reached for a pink one and crunched it. He smiled. Probably the cereal tasted good.

"Where's an orange one? Can you find an orange one?"

He pointed to one, scooped it up, and put it in his mouth.

"You ate it!" I acted surprised. "I wanted to eat it. Can you get *me* an orange one?"

He picked up another orange one and fed it to me.

"Yummy! Now, what color is this?" I picked up a purple one.

He wasn't tricked. He said nothing. Nothing, nothing. But he looked like he was giving the matter some thought. I finished my last spoonful and went to get a plastic bowl for Lucca. I filled it with cereal, poured in a little milk, and gave him a toddler spoon.

"Do you like the cereal?" Lucca's swinging feet told me he did.

He finished but stayed put, looking at me. I poured him another bowl.

Wait, I reminded myself. *Wait*. It was up to him.

• • •

Sam called that morning.

"Want to go to the amusement park? We're supposed to have bad weather, so maybe the lines will be short. We can wait out the storms at the carousel if they happen."

"Sure."

"Morgan's coming, too."

"Okay."

"We'll come get you in half an hour."

I dressed, got some money from Dad, and waited by the front porch.

Sam's dad drove us there and said he would come back for us at six p.m. That gave us loads of time—probably enough to go on every ride, because it wasn't the biggest amusement park. But it had a couple of roller coasters and it looked pretty fun.

Morgan and Sam both seemed to like roller coasters the way I do. You always have to sit in pairs, so I was worried about who should sit with who, but Sam was a born diplomat. He alternated sitting with each of us and then saying he wanted the seat to himself, making us sit together. Morgan seemed fine with the whole thing.

One ride was nauseating to watch. The riders stood up and held on to some vertical handles, and then the ride flipped them upside down and twisted them around in every direction at random.

"Cool!" Sam yelled.

Morgan and I looked at each other as Sam ran to get in line. "We're getting ice cream!" Morgan called after him. "Come on," she said to me. She got strawberry and I got coffee.

"It feels cooler now that I'm eating ice cream," I said.

"No way. It's blazing hot."

The thunderstorms hadn't come through yet. We headed back over to the crazy ride. Sam was still in line. We waved to him and then found a bench across the sidewalk so we could watch.

"I'm probably going to be sick just watching that thing," I said, slowing down my ice cream eating.

"Sam can be crazy," Morgan said. "But he says you're a crazy one, too."

My cheeks burned pink. "He said that? What did he say?"

"He said you talk to ghosts or something. Do you? You talk to ghosts?"

I shook my head. "Not really." There. Choose the vaguest words possible. Don't give a solid answer to anything. That's safest.

"Sam has the nuttiest ideas sometimes. That's too bad, though. I would have wanted to see that."

If she thought Sam's ideas were nutty, she wasn't likely to take any of the things he'd told her too seriously. Not that it didn't sting to know he'd been blabbing about something so private. I kept my cool, which wasn't too hard with the ice cream. "What, like have a séance?"

Morgan shrugged. "I don't know. It would be fun, like for Halloween. We could still do it. Get a lot of kids going."

"Does Sam really think I'm crazy?"

Morgan got a sly look. "Maybe. But I also know he thinks you're awesome. He doesn't shut up about you."

"Is that . . . okay with you?"

"Yeah, whatever!" She smiled.

"You mean you're not boyfriend and girlfriend?"

"No!" Morgan started laughing. "Sam's like my brother. We've been playing in the mud at the beach together since before we could walk."

"But even if he's just your friend . . . you don't mind . . . if he . . . or if I . . . ?"

Morgan shook her head. She gave her cone a good

chomp. When she was done chewing, she said, "I have a boyfriend, anyway. I haven't told Sam."

"Really? Why not?"

"Just easier. And he's been spending a lot of time with you, so he hasn't noticed I've been around less. For now, it's perfect until I want to tell him."

"Someone from school?"

"High school. He's a sophomore."

"Morgan!"

She grinned as she finished her ice cream cone.

Sam was leaving the ride. I hadn't even noticed that he'd had his turn. Just as I realized ice cream was running down my wrist like I was four years old, I noticed that Sam looked rather green. He stopped and bent over. Uh-oh.

"I got this." Morgan hopped up, ran over to him, and got him to sit down with his head between his knees. Soon Sam was looking a little better.

I realized that Morgan had just given me a secret to hold. Sarah's words drifted into my brain: *Ooh, a secret. Those special words that give you a tiny piece of someone else to carry around, to prove you know something important about them.*

I knew then that Sam wasn't my only friend up here. Even if I could talk to ghosts. Or whatever.

24

On Saturday, Mom and Dad thought the air was a good temperature for painting, so they were on ladders working on the outside of the house. I didn't like them up on ladders; I kept picturing them toppling and ending up paralyzed.

No sense staying home all day feeling nervous.

I found Lucca parked in his red and yellow Little Tikes car.

"Come on, kid, let's go to the park."

It was a bit of a walk, but Lucca only had to do some of it, because I gave him piggybacks off and on.

Nobody was at the playground. That was nice. I sat on a bench and Lucca ran around and climbed on things. Then he went over to the swings and needed help hopping onto a seat. I gave him a boost and started pushing him.

My mind kept wandering out toward the ocean. You could see it from here, too. From everywhere, it felt like.

The ocean. Now, that was something that kept going no matter how hard life got. And if I thought about it from standing right here, there seemed to be no end to it. On and on and on, no matter what happened.

"Higher!"

"Sorry," I said, remembering to give him a gentle shove.

"Higher!" He added, "Please."

Then I realized.

I ran around to the front of the swing and caught him. I hugged him and hugged him and hugged him.

"What?" Lucca didn't like this interruption. Who cared? I gave him a big kiss on the cheek. Then I calmed down. Didn't want to scare him. Didn't want to make too big a deal out of it and have him change his mind.

I went back to pushing him on the swing. I pushed him high, as he had asked, my arms never getting tired.

He was quiet.

But that was okay. It was something. It was a start.

• • •

When we got back to the house, I found Mom in the kitchen. She was eating strawberry yogurt right out of the big container with a huge spoon.

"You would never know that painting is so, so tiring." She leaned against the counter. "I'm beat."

"Too beat to even get a bowl?"

Lucca had followed me into the kitchen. "Go potty," I told him. He ran off to the bathroom.

217

Then I looked Mom right in the eyes.

"What?" she asked. "You going to get on my case about the bowl?"

"He said something!" I whispered.

Mom looked at me. She let the spoon fall into the yogurt. "No."

"He did! At the park! He said 'Higher,' for me to push him higher, on the swing. And he said 'Please.'"

Mom continued to stare into my eyes, to see if I was pulling her leg. Then she set the yogurt down and started crying.

"Are you sure?"

Hmm. I have been prone to visions and hallucinations. . . .

"Yes. Yes, I'm sure."

"I'll let your dad know—unless you want to, you're the one who heard him."

"You can tell him."

She squeezed my shoulders and gave me a little shake before she ran out of the room. I hoped she didn't knock Dad off a ladder or anything.

• • •

It was not instant, the change in Lucca. It wasn't like he would talk all the time. Mom and Dad waited, and I waited, for it to happen again.

Not another peep for about a week. Then one night Lucca seemed to think he was done eating, but he hadn't touched his peas at all. Usually he eats his peas. I even think they are one of his favorite things. But he wouldn't touch them and started to get pouty.

"Eat your peas," Mom said absentmindedly.

"No," said Lucca.

We all looked at him.

"No," Lucca said. "They are too squishy."

Mom and Dad leapt out of their chairs, jumped up and down, and ran to hug him.

Lucca looked embarrassed. He caught my eye as if to ask, *What's all the fuss about?*

• • •

The next afternoon, Lucca and I waited for Sam on the porch. When he appeared in the yard and came up the steps, he said, "Hey, Siena. Hey, Lucca."

I waited, smiling. Maybe Lucca would say something. It had been really, really hard to keep Lucca's talking a big secret from Sam. But I wanted Lucca to tell him himself, when he was ready.

"Hey, Sam!" Lucca shouted.

Sam looked stunned. But he collected himself, as if this wasn't a big deal at all—a totally different response from everyone in my family, and one Lucca needed, I bet. He said, "Hey, pal. Let's go get out that train set."

And Lucca ran off into the house.

Sam and I smiled at each other for a minute. I reached up and gave him a kiss on the cheek.

"Thank you," I whispered.

"No problem," he said. "See you after train time?"

• • •

I decided that—for once—I felt like brushing my hair and my teeth before dinner. And I checked that my clothes were clean and that they didn't look stretched out from wearing them all day. I tried on the lip gloss again. Then, when playtime was ending, I bounded down the stairs. Perfect: Sam was just setting all the "crashed" trains back on the tracks.

"There's time to go outside before dinner," I said.

"Okay. Look, we did a sock swap." Sam held out his foot. There was a tiny green-striped sock that barely squeezed onto his toes. I looked at Lucca, who had a much-too-big black sock bunched around his ankle.

"We traded socks!" Lucca explained.

"That's great," I laughed.

"See ya later, bud," Sam said to Lucca, who waved goodbye.

After we got off the porch, I said, "You can give me his sock back. I'll sneak it into the wash and he won't know."

"Nah, a promise is a promise. I'll just keep it in my pocket for now."

The little green sock disappeared into his pocket. A warm feeling rose in my chest. *Thank you, Sam. Thank you for caring so much about my brother.*

25

That night, I went to my room, unbelievably happy.

My thoughts went to Sarah. I hadn't tried to enter her story with the pen since I'd gone inside her without it. But I needed to see, to know, how it worked out for her. For one last time, I got out the pen.

I sat in the living room, flipping through one of Mama's magazines. There were a lot of neat craft projects I wanted to try. Maybe Mama would do them with me. She'd had time to spend with me lately.

She seemed to be doing a lot better. We all were.

I was still looking at the magazine when Jezzie arrived.

"Hello, Jezzie." I hadn't looked up, but I knew she'd jumped about a mile. I hadn't spoken to her in more than a year.

"Did I scare you?" I tossed the magazine onto the sofa as I stood up.

"No," she said, a little shaky. "How—how is Joshua today?"

"Not that you really care. You should go home. And not come back."

I walked her to the door.

"But—but—"

I gave her a look. "I mean it. Never come back here."

"But what about when my parents are coming . . . like at Christmas?"

"You'll have a cold. A really awful cold. And a stomachache."

"You want me to pretend to be sick any time my family is going to come here?"

"Oh, you won't pretend. When you think about coming here, your stomach will get all churny and your head will get all hot. Just because I say so. Just like you decided I wouldn't talk because you didn't want me to."

Jezzie looked angry. "I wouldn't want to be anywhere I'm not welcome." She looked back at me from the bottom porch step. "How did you come to talk again?"

"Joshua asked me to."

I shut the door and went back to my magazine.

Joshua joined me on the couch. He moved slowly these days; we learned that he had been very sick with a high fever that made strange things happen in his brain. It took him a long time to even recognize us, to remember our life together. But he made sure to spend time with me every day; sometimes we talked and sometimes we just played checkers.

"What are you looking at?" he asked.

"Mama's sewing magazine. Do you like these?" I showed him a picture. "Little sachets with potpourri in them. You put them in your bureau to make your clothes smell nice."

"You can make them for everyone at Christmas. Then everyone will smell good."

He had a book to read. "What's that?" I asked.

"A book about medicine. I think I might want to study that, medicine."

"To be a doctor?"

"Sure. To help people."

"Won't you have to go away again? I don't want you to go away again."

"Not the same way. I would just go to a university. Nearby."

I considered. "That might be all right."

"And not for a while. My own doctors won't let me go anywhere until I'm strong enough."

"Good." I leaned against him as he started to read. "I'm glad you came back."

I slept very late and woke to find a beautiful morning: sky clear and blue, leaves bright and green, water sparkling.

I thought about going to Mrs. Lang's, to ask her again what her friend had said about the people who lived in my house. Would she have something different to say now?

Then I realized: I had something myself—I had Sarah's report card!

I got it from the shelves with my collection. I turned it over to look at the teacher's comments.

The writing had changed!

Most of it was just about her academics now, but the very first sentence stood out: *Sarah is a lively member of our class, and she makes friends easily.* None of the sections mentioned her not speaking at all!

It had been real, my intervention, as real as what this report card had shown before. I had changed something. Something that mattered.

• • •

I went downstairs for breakfast to find Mom and Dad at the table surrounded by flyers and pamphlets.

"What are these?" I asked.

"Preschools."

Aw! It was finally time for Lucca to go to school!

I picked up a pamphlet. Cheerful toddlers using bright, primary-color paint. I figured they were staged, because when little kids paint, the colors don't stay separate for very long.

"His sentence structure is well beyond his age," Mom

said. "Maybe we should be looking into full-time school rather than a couple days a week. He'll be four before school starts."

"Maybe," Dad agreed. "We could have him tested again, see how it goes now that he talks."

"No!" I burst out.

Both of my parents stared at me.

"I . . ." I couldn't think of exactly how to explain. "Just let him be four."

They kept staring at me for a minute. Mom looked like she was about to be outraged, but Dad exchanged a calming look with her and kicked out a chair for me.

"Come help us look," he invited. "What you think is important, too."

I looked through the pamphlets with them. "This one sounds good." I held up a flyer. About twenty kids and held in a church basement; every day they had story time and music and, outside, playground time and nature walks. I could picture Lucca there, with other little kids, having fun. In fact, I saw it so clearly, I would say it was the first time I saw the future. "This one sounds right."

• • •

Later, Sam arrived at the front door.

"Get Lucca," he suggested.

I gave Sam a hug. Then I yelled down the hallway, "Lucca! Come on! We're going out!"

First we wandered through the wooded area on the ridges above the water, farther than I had been before. Sam and I took turns giving Lucca piggybacks. During one of his turns, Sam went running along the path, charging ahead, Lucca screaming with laughter as he was jostled up and down.

Then I remembered something.

"Hey, can we make a stop?"

I led the way back past our house and on to Mrs. Lang's.

"There you are!" she cried when she opened the door. "And Lucca, and . . ."

"Sam," all three of us finished.

"Are you . . . ?" Mrs. Lang studied Sam carefully. "Of Nielly's?"

"Yep!" said Sam.

"Oh, I know Sam Nielly. Who doesn't? Come in, come in!"

We followed her in.

"You know, I was making a big pasta salad to eat all week, but now that you've shown up, I think a meal with company might be nicer. Would you like some?"

We said yes and sat at the kitchen table. She served four bowls of pasta.

"Looks good!" Sam said.

"It does, Mrs. Lang," I agreed.

"Tastes good, too." Sam had already dug into his.

"Look," said Lucca. "I see peas, broccoli, and cheese."

"Are you going to eat the peas?" I asked.

"Today they are the yummiest." And Lucca happily popped a couple into his mouth with his fingers.

"I told you," Mrs. Lang said softly. "All in good time, right?"

"Right." Then I remembered why I'd wanted to see her. "Mrs. Lang, did you ask your friend Ella Mae about our house?"

"Oh, yes, I forgot to tell you! Ella Mae said that there was a family who lived there, a girl and a boy, back in the thirties and forties, before it became a place for vacationers."

I nodded.

"And when I told her you thought the house was haunted, she said she didn't know why that would be. She never heard of anything unusual there. The family went through some tough stuff during the war, but most families did. The children grew up and moved away."

I thought for a few minutes. Mrs. Lang looked at me; Sam looked at me; even Lucca looked at me.

Then I asked, "Lucca, are there still ghosts in the house?"

He shook his head. And then he said, "No. No more ghosts."

"I don't think there ever were," I realized slowly. "I think it was just feelings, the sadness that was left over. It's gone now."

We finished eating and helped with the dishes. Mrs. Lang and I washed them and the boys dried them at the table. Standing at the sink near the windowsill, I looked over the little plants and treasures there and felt a pang of guilt.

"I took something from you," I said to Mrs. Lang. "A little cup. I'm sorry. I'll bring it back."

She looked confused for a moment; then she remembered. "Oh, that. No matter, really. I haven't thought of it since. I'm glad you came to visit today."

We played a game of Memory. Lucca won every round again. Then we left, waving goodbye to Mrs. Lang from the fence.

Back on the beach, Lucca dropped to roll in the sand. Maybe it seemed like playing in the snow, because, again and again, he lay on his back like we'd taught him to do last winter in the park, spreading his arms and legs to shape figures, getting up carefully. "Angels," he said. "The beach is all filled up with angels."

"It is," I agreed. That was our Lucca, Mr. Shining and Bright. "Sam, is it okay if I walk by myself for a little bit?"

"Sure. We'll play right here."

I walked until I couldn't see them anymore, though I would come back soon. I wouldn't risk getting lost from them.

It was time, like Mom had said, for me just to be Siena. To not worry about Lucca, or how Mom and Dad felt about Lucca. Or to let images and visions and unexpected things unsettle me. Unexpected things could even be good. Like Sam. I hadn't expected a friend like him.

I could let the visions go for a while, now that I was in

control of them. I couldn't wait to travel the world and find out what I could see in new places, whose lives I could share. I knew my future also held the past, and all those places and people I would discover were already a part of me and I was of them. But first, it was time just to be myself and think about the things that I was and wanted to be.

I came across a small doll, a soft fabric doll, stained from being left in the water and sand.

I picked her up, turned her over. Where had she come from, and where was she going?

Not with me. I had everything I needed. I would leave her here. She wasn't going to be lonely. She had the sand and the water, the sun and the other stars, the blue sky of day and the wide dark of night . . . the whole universe. And she would melt back into it, and that would be okay.

It all started with a Scarecrow

Puffin is over seventy years old.
Sounds ancient, doesn't it? But Puffin has never been
so lively. We're always on the lookout for the next big
idea, which is how it began all those years ago.

Penguin Books was a big idea from the mind of
a man called Allen Lane, who in 1935 invented
the quality paperback and changed the world.
**And from great Penguins, great Puffins grew,
changing the face of children's books forever.**

The first four Puffin Picture Books were hatched in 1940 and the
first Puffin story book featured a man with broomstick arms called
Worzel Gummidge. In 1967 Kaye Webb, Puffin Editor, started the
Puffin Club, promising to **'make children into readers'**.
She kept that promise and over 200,000 children became devoted
Puffineers through their quarterly instalments of *Puffin Post*.

Many years from now, we hope you'll look back and
remember Puffin with a smile. **No matter what your age
or what you're into, there's a Puffin for everyone.**
The possibilities are endless, but one thing is for sure:
whether it's a picture book or a paperback, a sticker book
or a hardback, **if it's got that little Puffin
on it – it's bound to be good.**